ERSATZ EDEN

Ersatz Eden

Mind Your Own Garden

Jay & Mitsuko Miller

authorHOUSE®

AuthorHouse™
1663 Liberty Drive
Bloomington, IN 47403
www.authorhouse.com
Phone: 1-800-839-8640

First published by AuthorHouse   9/23/2009

ISBN: 978-1-4490-1145-1 (sc)

Printed in the United States of America
Bloomington, Indiana

This book is printed on acid-free paper.

Original Manuscript, Copyright 2009, by Jerry Miller
Los Angeles, California   Grumpy736@msn.com

CONTENTS

Front cover art – Yin & Yang Koi Pond

Ersatz Eden

Ersatz Eden

by Jay G. Miller

My late husband's unpublished novel has surfaced after thirty years. At his request back then I inserted a few comments into his account of a midlife crisis but soon lost interest. His fantasy life was not my cup of tea. The decades may have rendered it less amusing or they may have provided an interesting patina. I know it was not intended to be so, but reading it again after so many years it appears to be a pathological study in ambiguity, or maybe not.

Mitsuko Moriyama Miller, 2009

Preface

My father was Burt Lancaster and my mother was Lucille Ball. Dad was a tall muscular athlete who could walk on his hands for great distances. Mom says they first met when he passed by her on a sidewalk hand walking with his feet where his head should be.

Dad always spoke smoothly and authoritatively and although he was sociable he didn't seek the company of other men for idle conversation or team sports. You would mark him as a loner only if you didn't know him. He could be content focused on some project by himself or working within a group.

Mom dressed pretty much like Lucy in that popular TV show, had regular permanents with short bangs, and her best friend was our landlady. Those two ladies had a circle of giggling gals for gossip and bunko or canasta card games. There was always a lot of laughter around her. She played piano and sang the latest hit songs around the house.

Friends and relatives are not decided over which one I favor. Whatever, I've never experienced the 'was I adopted?' conundrum.

I'm proud to suggest that my visage fairly resembles Mike Farrell of M.A.S.H. I'm not as tall, though. He and Alan Alda are over six feet and I'm just barely five eleven.

We lived about two hundred miles down river from Minnesota's Twin Cities in the Tri-Cities, known today as the Quad-Cities. Some locals refer to it as the Quint-Cities. These towns are on both the Iowa and Illinois sides of the Mississippi River.

Dad worked at the International Harvester Farmall plant in Rock Island after learning welding from an uncle who worked at John Deere in Moline. Both companies produced millions of tractors, plows and other farm implements to the world.

The colonial French influence is still around subtly in many place names. The city of Moline derives its name from the French word for mill -- *moulin*. The name LeClaire graces the best hotel and movie theater in that city. When I learned that *haute cuisine* means high class food I deduced that Terre Haute means high ground. *N'est pas?*

Father Marquette paddled a canoe down the Mississippi in the 1600s. One of my teachers said that a monkey arriving on a ship from the Eastern Hemisphere in the 1600s could climb a tree on the Atlantic Shore and make its way all the way to the Mississippi River without touching ground. When I joined Sea Scouts I paddled a canoe on that same river and noticed how the trees reached out over the river banks in a few places that civilization had never touched. I still find it hard to believe that the monkey was able travel a thousand miles of wilderness without being frustrated by hundreds of creeks and rivers, though. Surely some of them would be too wide.

On my mother's side I found one French ancestor in my great-greats, so that would qualify me as one thirty-second Gallic, eh? On my father's side I have an indigenous ancestor among the great-greats, a female of the Tuckahoe tribe, affiliated with the Mohawk Nation. In the 50s there was a brief fad for young boys to sport Mohawk haircuts. I resisted the temptation. Had I been one-sixteenth I might have been tempted. Ethnic claims need to be one-sixteenth to be valid, not one-thirty-second or so I've been led to understand.

Descendents of the Sauk-Fox tribes hold annual powwows at Blackhawk State Park in the Quad-Cities, specifically Rock Island. Their final hostilities were against Captain Abraham Lincoln who captured them without bloodshed with a volunteer unit. Abe was captain because he could out wrestle any man in the group.

After completing my military service without bloodshed I mustered out at Camp Pendleton and stayed in California to go to college, marry and settle down in the Los Angeles area. Everyone was doing it. It was practically the thing to do.

Pat Brown was governor, junior college was free and they even sent school buses to pick us college students up on the street by our homes. I abandoned my previous plan to use the G.I. Bill at Beloit College in Wisconsin. Once in awhile I get a twinge of regret over that but what has been, has been. I don't know the Italian past tense equivalent of *que sera, sera* or I would have said it instead of has been, has been. The French term *fait accompli* doesn't really fit either.

I like to throw in little foreign idioms as compensation for never really learning any other language fluently. There is an English word for exaggerating one's erudition, but I've forgotten that word, hence this awkward, long explanatory digression. While we're on the subject let me confess right out that my I.Q. in college was only 120. Since then I have lost quite a few points.

Allow me to suggest that some of the following material may puzzle the reader as inconsistent or contradictory. As the story unfolds such surface impressions should be dispelled.

In the first chapter I back away from cigarette smoke. In the second chapter I light up a cigar. That may be inconsistent to some people but it is my true nature. Cigarette smoke makes me physically sick. At the same time the smell of a fine cigar is perfume to my nose. Since I don't inhale them, I enjoy puffing on one every time the Cubs win the pennant or whenever a Democratic President of the United States is inaugurated.

Also, the tone in the narrative makes me sound like a bachelor because I've only written about things that I did apart from my wife when she was out of town. All during the time of this story I was a married man and my wife was a very great and most enjoyable part of my life. I'm stressing the importance of my marriage because I'm about to relate a tale of temptation. Maybe I could exaggerate the temptation just a bit for drama. President Carter says he lusted in his heart. So do 99 and 44/100 percent of men every hour every day. It's beyond our control. Yeah, that's it. Mitsuko: this is a fictional spin, OK?

For that reason, I've asked my wife to look over the manuscript in the word processor and insert comments or clarifications as she feels warranted. This commentary should be differentiated from my narrative in some manner so the reader can distinguish her comments from my mine. This has been done before. The team of Will and Ariel Durant is but one example. Most of all I want her to vouch for some of the events that you might take as exaggerations. I trust my wife and she has always trusted me.

Jay G. Miller, October, 1979

Jay has many faults such as being excessively opinionated but to my knowledge prevarication for his advantage has never been one of them. His working title was MIND YOUR OWN BUSINESS which I thought too prosaic until I read the manuscript. Still, I changed it.

Mitsuko Moriyama Miller December, 1979

Chapter One

April

It was a beautiful April afternoon in Malibu. The clear blue sky made the Pacific Ocean bluer than usual. The manicured lawns and gardens of the rich were green from precisely measured organic fertilizers and regular applications of water sprinklers in conjunction with heavenly sponsored sunshine and gentle temperatures; God and man working together to create an Eden.

My father used to talk like that. He was more religious than I am and he gave me a lot of good advice that I didn't recognize as wisdom at the time. He died last year of the combined effects of a weak heart and cancer at age sixty-seven.

There were three of us manning the gate at a political fundraiser on a Malibu estate on a hill overlooking the ocean. A matronly lady from Chatsworth sat at a card table taking donations and selling drink tickets. A young political science major from UCLA with a five-day beard was her volunteer assistant. As the tallest and beefiest of the three, and as an ex-marine, I assumed the role of sergeant at arms. I stood in the middle of the open gated driveway directing pedestrian traffic over to the sign-in table with my 'Hello, My Name is Jay' badge of authority.

If I hadn't volunteered to work this Sunday afternoon garden party I would be in the pool back at my apartment in Beverly Hills enjoying the April sunshine. Even if I didn't need the exercise I liked to check out the lady swimmers from the other apartments. I admit it proudly. Behind my façade of stoic disinterest I'm a compulsive admirer of feminine pulchritude.

> MMM: Pretension! He's led off the story by living in Beverly Hills! It's legitimate but misleading. We've only lived here the past seven years since I began teaching at UCLA, and it is a small rented *pied-a-terre* south of Olympic Boulevard. We are far from well off.

April is the beginning of the warm weather swim season. Most swimming pools around here get a lot of attention when the cooler weather of November through March is over. Some people swim year round, of course, but my own regimen is to swim only from April through October. The story that I'm about to commit to paper here also takes place from April to October this year. I'm sure it's purely coincidental. I only noticed it when I outlined the chapters to be typed.

I've been to a lot of these political garden parties before and was fairly well known in the local activist scene. My reputation was well established enough to be named treasurer of a couple of progressive groups.

The memory I treasure most in this area was an evening cocktail party with Rod Serling and his wife years ago at his home in Pacific Palisades. He was lending his name to a cause as honorary membership chairman and several of us actual chapter membership chairpersons were invited to his house. When he introduced his wife he said, "The mortgage here is in her name." I thought that was an odd thing to say, but he died a few years later so maybe he knew something.

While we are on the subject of political garden parties I would like to mention that I've had opportunities to attend one or two of Hugh Hefner's Holmby Hills soirees, but passed them up. Not even idle curiosity could induce me to check out his palatial pad. The required donations were pretty steep, but I've paid more for similar events that I believed in.

> MMM: I've chosen to edit out several hundred words about the Playboy Empire and its effect on American culture. Jay could have boiled it down to 'hedonism is pleasure without conscience, women of easy virtue are not attractive, and photos of bare skin are cheesy attention gimmicks.' He went on endlessly and it is hard to tell if he was denigrating or envying Mr. Hefner. I am editing, not censoring.

On this April Sunday afternoon we three gatekeepers were thrown into some confusion when Jane Fonda and her entourage walked up to our table and she proffered cash for tickets of admission. We should have refused it since she was billed as the Guest of Honor but we each looked at each other blankly and spinning wheels inside our heads did not engage.

By the time I came up with, 'she's the guest of honor, but maybe she could pay for her entourage' it was too late. Mrs. Pritchard had already taken the money and given her tickets for all. She then offered a couple of quick pleasantries of admiration but Jane was distracted by a young child holding her hand and she didn't respond.

It was my first time seeing Miss Fonda in person and she looked just the same in three dimensions as she does in two. Many stars don't. I'd met her father and he also had the same quality in three dimensions. So did James Whitmore and Walter Matthau. John Ritter is not the same as what you see on TV. For one thing he's taller than the average man, and is very freckled. John Denver was also taller than I expected. Possibly even six feet! We were in the front rows at his Irvine Meadows concert.

The host and hostess came hurrying down the driveway having spotted Jane Fonda from some vantage point up on their estate. Other people followed the hosts down the driveway, so as Miss Fonda went up the hill she and her entourage were surrounded by enthusiastic partisans.

In retrospect the hosts should have arranged for someone on the street to watch for her and then to direct her car to proceed on up to the top. Come to think of it, they might have expected me to do that, but I didn't see the car. She just came walking from the street as all the other guests had done. Maybe Jane and her group had taken a taxi or someone had dropped them off. Possibly it wasn't my fault, but I'll accept the blame for the snafu regardless. I'm not here to make excuses.

Later when proceedings were underway up in the garden and the stragglers were few and far between we three gatekeepers began discussing a rotation whereby one or two of us could join the party. Just then a group of five people came scurrying up the driveway. They swung wide around me as if they knew they were late and had to hurry not to miss anything. One of them was an older man in a wheel chair. Three younger men that could have been his sons, and a young woman, possibly a daughter-in-law, trailed along with him. I shouted 'Hey, over here!' for them to hold it, to register at the table before proceeding in.

Tickets were ten dollars. It's a nominal amount for an affair of this kind. I've been to many that were more expensive. Access to the *hors d'oeuvres* trays up there at the house alone was worth more than ten dollars. The old man took out his wallet as if to comply and then said,

"Doggone, son, I'm an old crippled man. I can't afford fifty dollars or even ten dollars for this meeting. Why do we have to pay?"

"It isn't a public meeting. It has been advertised as a fundraiser at a private home," I insisted.

The other four took to complaining very, very loudly, shouting even though we were standing nose to nose.

"Hey! We are poor people! Surely you aren't going to charge poor people to see Jane Fonda! Why can't poor people see Jane Fonda?" Ridiculous non sequiturs.

The commotion got so loud a couple of politicos up at the house came down to see what the ruckus was about. My two fellow greeters were now opposing my decision, suggesting we just let them in without donating. It wasn't going to hurt anything or make any difference, they said.

I wasn't born a laid back Californian. I am mostly presbyterian scots-irish from the mid-west. We believe in formalities, not anything goes or seat-of-the-pants decision making. We don't cotton to freeloaders who cry poor mouth in the middle of Malibu. If they couldn't afford the advertised ten dollars, then why get dressed up and drive over to a private political fundraiser? I resisted the crashers and my two colleagues until those two politico sponsors from up the hill that had responded to the loud scene said,

"Oh, just let them in. It's all right."

So I stepped aside. I paid for my ticket, and was missing most of the entertainment up there on the hill. Jane Fonda paid for her ticket. But oh-no, no-oh, these five loudmouth bellyachers had to be accommodated for free. I put my hands behind my back and stepped aside but pointedly refused to say 'OK' or 'all right, then.'

Of course the five crashers proceeded to load up with free food, and then became loud, rude, disruptive hecklers interrupting the speakers. They made pests of themselves. I felt vindicated. No wonder those right wing interlopers didn't want to pay for admission.

Many days later I analyzed the situation. There were five people wanting to get in free, two admissions people were willing to let them in free, and one stiff necked guy was opposed. To those two politicians that's seven to one. Seven wins. The issue of right or wrong is not even considered for a moment. That's what's gone wrong with this country. Right or wrong should matter. It should at least be considered.

As luck would have it I was living in Beverly Hills at the time and my wife and I hosted little political activist discussion groups once in awhile at our small apartment in the flats, south of Wilshire Boulevard where some of the less affluent people live.

We were on Bedford Drive just four blocks south of Neiman-Marcus which is across Wilshire from Carroll O'Connor's saloon, The Ginger Man Restaurant. In the opposite direction it's almost around the corner from Twentieth-Century Fox Studios on Pico where M.A.S.H. interiors are filmed.

I read an interview with Alan Alda where he said that he commuted to his New Jersey home on weekends but rented an apartment near the studio to use during the week while filming and writing scripts for the show. It well could have been on Bedford Drive.

It was a convenient location for my wife, Dr. Mitsuko Moriyama, an instructor in the French patois over at UCLA. I hoped the prestige of the address would give me some credibility with her family. She's from an aristocratic clan who believe she married beneath her station to a dreaded *iyashi gaijin*.

Their family doctor, for example, was the emperor's family doctor. Mitsi's father served in the diplomatic corps in Paris and Geneva long enough for her to be more fluent in French than in English. I met her on campus soon after mustering out of the marines and luck seemed to favor me ever since.

> MMM notation: My husband has a big mouth. When I told him about having the same physician as the emperor it was just a tiny detail about an illness and

I wasn't passing myself off as aristocratic. My family was just lucky in attending the right schools, a tradition of serving in the government, and in owning property in Tokyo that skyrocketed in value after the war. We are only a samurai clan, not aristocrats.

One thing mid-westerners know is how to mind our own business. It seemed to me, over the course of working in several places, and a couple decades into it, that no matter where you work there are cliques. By not being a joiner, by being a listener, and by avoiding expressing an opinion that takes sides, people just assumed I was in their clique, and they would tell me things, confidential things I really didn't need to hear.

Where I just said I avoided expressing an opinion, it was overstating the case. Most times I had no opinion. Over the years I've learned to reserve judging an event until more than one person has been heard from, or until time has lent some perspective. I rarely offer an agreeable expletive because I've found that sometimes stories are exaggerated for the sole purpose of provoking expletives. I wait while weighing whether or not any response is appropriate or necessary.

This was most noticeable in the marines. The guys in the barracks would tell the wildest stories to entertain their bunkmates about their exploits. I always held back my chuckle or credulity just a bit, but never in an obvious way. When I first noticed myself doing this, I was self critical. Was I being two faced? I despise two faced people. But when you live in a squad bay full of forty men where thirty-eight are pure b. s. artists and I'm not too sure about the thirty-ninth, my reactions were as honest as they could be in the circumstances, I swear.

At these parties that Mitsi and I went to or hosted, there would be some familiar faces. People would assume that I was of the same persuasion as they were, and then tell me things as if I was trusted family. Or maybe they just blabbed out everything they knew to everyone they met. Liquor may also be to blame. I like to think their candor derived from my attitude, my friendly, open, middle-American face.

This could be a good place to indicate that I consider myself to be trustworthy, loyal, helpful, friendly, courteous, kind, obedient, cheerful, thrifty, brave, clean, and reverent. I put that on a job application once and was hired for a financial holding company based on the corner of Wilshire and Doheny.

It amuses me now to think that a financial holding company would actually hire a boy scout. Reflecting about that reminds me of Homer and Jethro's parody song about the Battle of New Orleans. *"A rooty toot toot, a rooty toot toot. We are the boys from the boy scout troop. We don't smoke and we don't chew, and we don't go with the girls that do."* In fact, I adopted a personal credo for those years before my marriage: Lips that touch tobacco shall never touch mine.

On my first day on the job the president of the company came to see my boss and said, "What were the earnings for last month?" My boss replied, "What do you want them to be?"

After that my boss showed me how to maintain three sets of books -- perfectly legal -- based on who the figures are for. One set for the board of directors, one set for the government, and one set of cash books with the unadorned, unmassaged truth. Just as an aside: some earnings were stashed in the balance sheet under reserves, but the board of directors wanted to see them recognized on the current profit and loss. Accounting is an art, not a science.

This particular party, the Jane Fonda garden party, was where I saw someone for the first time about whom this story was written. SHE was a stunning young lady sitting off to the side away from the rows of lawn chairs, reading a book, as if she wasn't present at the meeting to talk politics or listen to speakers. I noticed several young studs going over to talk to her, trying to get her to put her book down and join the party, but she would shake them off and bury her nose in the book again. I've decided to call her SHE in this narrative. I'll explain later.

As I said, it was April, and it was spring break. Mitsi had flown to Washington D.C. to visit an uncle and hopefully catch the cherry blossom season. I was batching it at our pad. I never, ever, flirt with girls. I think I was born a married man and never had that seven year itch or any other kind. It's not part of my personality to make a pass. The whole ritual is completely foreign to me and I wouldn't know how to do it even if someone scripted it for me and rehearsed me over and over how to play the part.

So, naturally, I went over to where she was trying to hide herself and gave her a pickup line like a professional make-out artist. Something like, "Hiii, can I buy this house for you?" I don't know why those words came out of my mouth. There was no thought or planning involved. My voice was acting independently of my conscious brain.

There may be some technical explanation for that. My brain was overwhelmed with sensory information and could not sort it out properly to advise my vocal chords and I know why. It's because SHE was the most awesome woman I'd ever seen in person.

I've seen the crème de la crème of Hollywood. I've seen them shopping at Neiman-Marcus and at the Century Plaza. I've seen them at the beach, in the supermarkets, in stage productions in non-equity theaters (in less than 99 seat capacity audiences you sit really close to the actors), in shootings of movies and television shows, as hostesses of business shows, as elegant receptionists and executive assistants in Century City.

My brother makes a modest living photographing lovely young ladies putting portfolios together for modeling or entertainment jobs. Please believe me when I say I've seen the cream of the cream of the *crème de la crème de la creme* in physical perfection, in various stages of dress and undress such as bikinis, lingerie, and underwear.

My wife and I once saw Judy Landers shopping at Century City. Mitsi just happened to be in the changing room when Judy tried on a dress. Later I had to bite my knuckle when she described what Judy was like under her street clothes.

MMM: True story

So when I say SHE knocked me over, please put it in context. She was special. She was young, fresh looking, impeccably attired, no makeup, no perfume, just a presence that stupefied me. She had intelligence in her eyes, and just the fact that she was reading intrigued me.

It was completely out of character for me to utter that ridiculous introduction. I plead temporary insanity. I've since learned that SHE does not flirt, is a one man woman, and 999,999 times out of 1,000,000 would pretend to not even hear such an outrageous gambit. Maybe it was my innocent face. Anyway, astonishingly, she picked up on the line and replied that she'd trade her soul for a house like this one.

Aha! An answer! A Faustian answer! What did that make me? Shame on me! I kept playing along. I pulled up a chair. As it turned out, she was there with the band. Her husband was playing drums and I noticed him glaring at me a couple of times as I sat beside his wife just chatting about life in general, the state of the world, popular entertainment, the usual b. s. It hadn't occurred to me that she'd be married. Don't misunderstand. She was an adult, fully developed and yet still looked as innocent as a child. She wore no ring, seemed shy and spoke quietly with a sexy foreign accent.

Now might be a good time to muse about the nomenclature: SHE. I've decided that disclosing her name would cheapen her impact within the context of this narrative. Epiphany: That must be why English speaking Christians use the Greek name Jesus rather than the Hebrew name Joshua or even Yeshua in mentioning the Christ. If our King James Bibles said: Joshua did this or that you already have a mental image of a person named Joshua. You have an image of Old Testament Joshua who was a heroic general who fought the battle at Jericho. You may personally know many contemporary men named Josh or Joshua. It trivializes the awesome personality of the one and only Son of God, Mary, and Joseph. He deserves a unique name.

But then there's no way I can explain why the Spanish speakers stick with the name Jesus, a Greek misspelling, mispronouncing, of Hebrew because they call their sons, fathers, uncles Haysoos. There are thousands of Haysooses in the Hispanic language world. Does that invalidate my theory about the English speaking world? You decide.

I considered assigning her some number nomenclature instead of alphabetic characters to indicate she was not of the known world. Ten squared? A new film suggests ladies can be appraised by numbers from one to ten. No, I don't play that game. It's too shallow. Beauty can be very superficial, as that film proved. No. Just trust me that this SHE for the purposes of this narrative was in a category of her own. Hey, she's fictional anyway, right? Cut me some slack.

I used to read a newspaper columnist who always referred to his wife as BW. I think it stood for Beautiful Wife. He'd write, "BW and I were at this supper club when--." No. Initials have been done to death especially for girls like BB, CC, DD, GG, JJ, (Bibi, CeeCee, DeeDee, Gigi, JayJay, etc). Double AA or Triple A is used for other quality purposes.

No, I had to devose a new code name -- SHE. When I capitalize all three letters, it's this special young lady's name for purposes of this story. The lower case 'she' can refer to this unique young lady or any other female in context.

Looking back at that paragraph it occurred to me that perhaps the reader recognizes my use of SHE is not original. My sister wears a fleece shirt that says SHE WHO MUST BE OBEYED. There have been two films with that title about a goddess leader in some Shangri-la area. The first one I saw was with Randolph Scott and Helen Gahagan, the actress that Richard Nixon smeared in his ruthless climb to power, and the newer one had Ursula Andress as SHE. Forgive me, but I've wracked my brain for nomenclature that sets the young lady apart. Nothing else works. I hope you aren't getting her name mixed up with the pronoun. I'm not sure I can torture every sentence that calls for her name to be inserted. I considered SHE within parentheses but that looked silly after the first few times so I dropped it.

SHE was at least fifteen years younger than Mitsi and me, possibly even twenty. Maybe that was part of the appeal. If she had to be married she was what any successful older man like me in his late thirties would call a trophy wife. She was someone to strut around proudly with, flaunting her for all to see.

> MMM: I don't know why my husband implies he's in his late thirties. He will be 42 in July.

During a band break we walked over and she introduced me to her husband. He didn't say anything. Maybe he could sense from the expression on my face that I was sizing him up as unworthy a mate for such a fine specimen of femininity. His attitude suggested 'Hey, dude, I'm just here for the money, not to socialize with you creeps.'

After he lit up a cigarette I backed off and wandered away. I can't tolerate the smell anymore. I felt terribly, terribly sorry for the beautiful girl for having to live with an insensitive nicotine addict. The smell would get into her hair and the carcinogens would get into her lungs.

Cigarette smokers should only marry cigarette smokers. Let the rest of humanity live! It must have been hell for her. Naturally I didn't say so out loud having a usual modicum of discretion. At more than one smoke filled meeting of progressive activists I've suggested that after we get more social justice we need to oppress the smokers because they are killing us slowly but surely with their side stream guck.

As much as I like music I've never found musicians to be worth a damn socially with us civilians. I don't know why that is. Perhaps they live in their own little niches with others of their species and regard the rest of the human race with contempt. Although, to be fair, sometimes I think our civilization deserves the contempt of its artists. They see the world differently, perhaps as it could have been or should be.

Events that occurred later confirmed what I always thought about drum players being the least mentally gifted members of bands or orchestras. I'm thinking now of the horn or reed players who sometimes sight read and transpose a key of music on the page to a different key that everyone is playing.

I played trombone in the Moline High School marching band. You may be thinking that I chose that instrument because of Glenn Miller. Well, partly. We both wore glasses, but my main reason was a popular tune at the time called Bonaparte's Retreat.

> *Well, I took in my arms I*
> *Told her of her many charms I*
> *Kissed her while the jazz band played*
> *The Bonaparte's Retreat*

Trombones can utilize a sliding note effectively and I liked that mellow sound in that song. I admired the skill of most musicians in our band and noticed that drummers at least possess a superior degree of practiced dexterity.

Still, I didn't respect them as I did the rest of the band members. The percussionists seemed one dimensional at least in my appraisals. Come to think of it, that may explain why Ringo has always garnered less respect than John, Paul, and George. The other three musicians are multifaceted composers and singers. Yes, George too! Ringo and I share the same birthday by the way.

The drummer was at least my age. And for some unfathomable reason he had this incredibly beautiful young wife. Yeah, maybe I'd be uneasy too. Maybe I'd try to keep all strangers beyond arms length. For is it not written: the beauty of a wife is not to be shared! Victor Mature said that in a sword and turban film once referring to Anita Ekberg after she performed a dance of the seven veils.

It was extremely lucky for me that her husband was there. I would not be called upon to put up or shut up on my buy you a house gambit. It was fun play acting the big shot this one time. I had pulled it off. No harm, no foul. Luckily also I'd worn my newest custom fitted suit since I was on the host's committee, with my one seventy five dollar silk necktie.

Remember Tony Curtis in The Defiant Ones? When he was exultant, on top of the world, he would exclaim: I'm Charley Potatoes! That was me. My brother had picked up that catch phrase and used it a lot when he was going out anywhere there would be champagne and beautiful girls. Now I know how he felt. Now I was Charley Potatoes!

An hour or so later, after the host thank-you-for-coming-and-drive-safely-benediction, SHE helped her husband load his drums into a van and they left. For a few moments it looked like I might be leaving at the same time as they were. I was on the clean up crew and was one of the last to leave. I momentarily worried that SHE would see me approaching the Volvo station wagon left in the driveway and driving it away. Sure, it's acceptable for transportation of the well off, but its silhouette practically insists that its owners are married with children. I quickly invented a cover story that I was driving my sister's car today for some reason or other.

I don't remember what any of the program was about that day because SHE and I sat it out and later I daydreamed about her after she left. I'd evidently pressed the right button, pretending to be filthy rich. She was married to a struggling musician all right but she was open to a suggestion or two from a millionaire. Even the most desirable woman is the same as the least desirable. Get the richest man you can find. The ladies are all alike.

Or was I being unfair? She had not started the conversation; I had. She was trying to keep a low profile and read her book. The things we talked about revealed a depth of character that would have made her beautiful even if she hadn't been born that way.

She gave the impression that she would have talked to me even if I hadn't offered that stupid comment. She never inquired what I did for a living or anything that might confirm my vast fortune. For example she never said, 'what kind of car do you drive?' or 'where do you work?' or 'where do you live?' or 'do you like to travel?'

She was self deprecating and modest and not at all self centered. She could talk about a subject and very, very infrequently use a personal pronoun, unlike myself, eh? She could have been a young Eleanor Roosevelt.

MMM: Can't comment. Maybe later after this barf coming up ---

I'm a good listener. I could have fallen in love under the right circumstances. It could easily have escalated into a full blown midlife crisis but it was never to be. She was married and I was married. I just found it interesting how you can feel like a schoolboy again so many years into maturity. I had never expected my adrenalin to go pumping like that ever again and there it was.

She had not flirted with me openly but I now believed that if I had offered it, we could have left the party and gone off in my luxury convertible to my fabulous pad atop the Beverly Wilshire, and then onto a whirlwind tour of Las Vegas, Hawaii, and Hong Kong, buying clothes and other items as we needed them. She had focused on me as if there was no party or husband there.

I flattered myself with speculation that pure ultimate paradise appeared attainable if only I had been born rich instead of so devilishly handsome. As the escort of the *numero uno* woman in the world, I would be the *numero uno* man. The richest tycoon, the most popular celebrity, the most powerful potentate would all envy me, Charley Potatoes.

People everywhere would ponder: who is this fellow who has on his arm the most desirable woman in the world. They would wonder what had qualified me to be the consort of the sexiest woman alive. As I said before, at the time, I didn't know she was a one man woman.

As they drove off I worried about her. Would her loutish husband punch her around for talking to me? Had he lit a cigarette and was even then destroying her lungs in their van? Maybe I should get my car and follow them and make sure she's all right. No, that might only cause trouble for her. Better to just treasure the feeling of the moment and file the memory of her forever as an almost conquest.

The party had started at 2 PM and ended at 6 PM. The *hors d'oeuvres* were supposed to tide you over until supper somewhere else. After all the appropriate goodbyes I climbed into my Volvo and drove home contemplating the events of the day. Someone there said to all of us departees, 'Be very kind to each other, will you?' That was Garry Moore's old sign off line, an odd thing to say but it might have been the theme of the party that I had missed.

I know for sure that neither Garry nor Durwood Kirby were there.

As I turned up Sunset, as I had a hundred times, I suddenly realized the boulevard is very aptly named. It runs from downtown Los Angeles right to the ocean where the sun actually sets. No, I had not ingested any hallucinogens or mind expanders. Sometimes I just get these obvious insights when I'm alone and my thoughts are rambling. Of course the actual placement of the sunset on the horizon changes with the earth's orbit, but still, the end of Sunset Blvd right there on the beach often places the setting sun almost directly ahead.

As the sun was sinking out over the Pacific it was sending shimmering gold reflections on the windows of the rich. It was so much like a cliché that I wished someone was in the car with me so I could say, Wow, looked at all the ephemeral gold on those windows! How many times do we get to use the word ephemeral in a sentence?' But I was alone with my inane thoughts. It was no use. SHE took over control of all my thoughts again.

I haven't begun to describe her beauty. Beauty is a subjective emotional reaction that does not lend itself to words. Advertisers and popular songwriters have debased our language. Back in the 20s or whenever great literature had its last gasp, the writers had an advantage over writers of this era.

Today's readers have been showered with a Niagara of words, especially pretty descriptive adjectives and metaphors from magazines, television, books, and films until we've been desensitized to them. Pathetic looking skinny waifs have been trotted out and hyped as if The Queen of Sheba, Helen of Troy, Cleopatra, and Josephine Beauharnais never existed.

At one time the Guinness Book of Records listed the most beautiful woman as voted by patrons of Madame Toussaud's Wax Museum in London. The number one choice for Most Beautiful Woman in the World was a thin young model named Twiggy. Does that give us a clue about subjectivity and the crowd that does the voting? Wouldn't you think that title was a bit pretentious for a wax museum in one little corner of a city to define? What chutzpah! Well, it is a tourist attraction in a major world city, so maybe not purely irrational, but still---

I read recently in a Sunday supplement about a woman writer's first impression of Omar Sharif in Doctor Zhivago. She wrote that he seemed the handsomest, sexiest man she'd ever seen. Later she read an interview where he said his life was devoted to playing bridge. The next time she saw him on the silver screen he wasn't so attractive. His eyes were rheumy, not wet-sexy brown. His chin wasn't shaped well. Things like that.

Appearances are shaped by our mood and not what we actually see. I've heard that neither Clark Gable nor Richard Gere were great shakes with the ladies in high school. Frank Sinatra's agents hired swooning bobby-soxers to lead other little girls into self induced excessive ecstasies. I can't think of the term -- Judas goat?

Popular idols had to be magnified up there on the screen, groomed and hyped by press agents. With men, toupees become useful. Maybe paste back the ears. Let's not even discuss cosmetic surgery. But remember the line from Hooray for Hollywood – *to be an actor see Mr. Factor, he can make a monkey look good.*

Beside all the hype words our modern world also has too many visual stimuli. Images on MTV are flashed at a fast pace because the station managers know the song is banal and trite and only its pace, energy, and quick juxtaposition of edited cuts can maintain an interest level for the two minutes it takes to run, keeping you tuned for the next commercial.

Having just reflected on that I still think you would agree with me that SHE was the most beautiful girl at least for that day in that setting, if you had been there.

I often shed tears at weddings because I am convinced by the ritual ceremony, the incantations, the music, the flowers aromas and the bride's dress that magic is happening, that the bride at that moment is indisputably the most beautiful woman in the world. No one could dare argue with me at that moment.

> MMM: True! He sheds tears at every wedding. I used to suspect they were tears of envy so I enjoyed reading this explanation that the moisture is from condensed sentiment.

I've mentioned there was not a trace of cosmetics or perfume on her. Would you gild a rose? Would you cover an Oreo cookie with chocolate? It can be done and it has been done, but why?

I could have fallen in love with her hair alone and I am most definitely not a fetishist. Her eyes were intelligent and lively, and her mouth? Well, I could kill men or charging beasts, if she would smile at me for doing so. She radiated innocence and youth. I could not imagine her smoking or drinking alcohol. She probably ate yogurt with the purest pureed fruits, drank only imported water from an Olympian mountain spring, and never even glanced at, let alone ingested, red meat.

It puzzles me about how we sometimes have that instant attraction, or instinctive impression, what used to be called chemistry. In adolescents we call it hormones. Whatever it is at my age I don't think I'm supposed to have it.

Instead of chemical could there be an intellectual or spiritual connection? What if there is such a thing as reincarnation? According to Shirley MacLaine we often meet the same people when we are reincarnated and sometimes have unresolved issues or passions that subconsciously guide our actions. Shirley is one of my ideal women in a sisterly kind of way. Mitsi and I are fans.

MMM: It's true. We both enjoy her films as well as her books.

What if in a previous life, SHE had been a princess in a palace and had died suddenly while too young. Maybe since she began this present incarnation she's been puzzled about where she is now. She had been comfortable being tutored by all the great teachers her emperor father could find. Maybe that's why she is searching for that palatial house of her dreams.

People who believe in reincarnation cite many instances of children up to the age of four that remember other lives in other places. After reaching three or four years the memories fade. His Holiness, the Dalai Lama at an early age recognized and claimed artifacts from his previous incarnation.

Dare we imagine she could have been the last Tsar's daughter Anastasia, brutally murdered with the rest of her family and impersonated by pretenders seeking her Romanoff inheritance? That is a fantasy scenario everyone has pondered, *n'est pas*?

My apologies for this digression. This was not intended to be a polemic on my beliefs about the world or the universe. Maybe you needed a bit of perspective on my point of view, though. Let me assure you that you will not be subjected to any further adolescent hallucinations of an almost middle aged codger.

I've controlled my fantasies pretty much. I treasure every waking moment with Mitsuko and I'm dismayed that at night, in sleep, we must go separate ways to dreamland. I'm supposed to spend seven or eight hours with my own unconscious imagination? Yuck.

Incidentally, if you didn't already know, mitsu means honey in her native tongue. 'Ko' is the feminine suffix. Mitsuko, Aiko, Yoko, Shoko, Shizuko, etc. We have a wonderful relationship and I would never do anything silly to sully that bond. She knows my daydreams are harmless.

MMM: I was going to comment, but I read ahead to the following, so I'll just let it speak for itself.

Once when we were waiting in line at RJ's for Ribs on Beverly Drive I looked out the window by the front door and was momentarily stupefied by a sensationally, disturbingly, awesomely, hot blond casually peering in the window as she window shopped up the street. She was dressed in finery from the best shops on Rodeo Drive and her hair was long and full of shiny highlights. You don't see that kind of hair outside of the glamour capitals. I don't know what it was about me, whether I had gone slack jawed or bug eyed, but I looked into her face and she smiled at me!

She continued her slow walk up the street and I watched for her to appear again at the next window, still following her steps with my eyes. She looked back at me with a confident smile that said, 'I knew you would be watching.'

Grace Kelly sickened me when she chose a faux prince of a faux state who derived his fortune from gambling. I was appalled at how empty headed she seemed at the time. Or, could it be, she had been a princess in a previous life, and longed for the splendor of a castle and the deference of servants and subjects? I saw her in that MGM movie The Swan, but this Monaco prince guy was no Louis Jourdan!

No matter, it still creeps me out to think of her married to a homely pudgy casino operator with a mustache and a pretentious title. Monaco is half the size of New York City's Central Park! His mother had been a washer woman and that's about the only positive thing in his favor in my opinion. At least his mother had been a wage earner and not a one hundred per cent parasite.

Grace Kelly's choice of mate will be the mystery of my lifetime, along with Linda Ronstadt's unchoice of a mate. Extremely well named Linda could have any man in the world she wanted, but evidently didn't want one permanently.

I'd also like to put in a word for Maria Muldaur. I'd like to approach her backstage at a concert sometime and say, "I'll bet you can't make a man out of me!" Cause she's a woman, W-O-M-A -N; she can make a dress out of a feedbag! She can make a man out of you!

SHE had only been in this country for six months when I met her. Her English was passable and she had enough vocabulary to discuss philosophy. Wherever she went to college, it was a good school with classical disciplines. She made a completely favorable impression on me is what I'm trying to say, an indelible impression, and I don't believe that I'm easily impressed.

> MMM: You can't imagine how much I've deleted in this first chapter. He had pages and pages of long passages that would convince anyone he suffered from yellow fever long before it became an epidemic here, long before Marlon Brando and John Lennon. His fever began in the 40s with The Dragon Lady in Terry and the Pirates and a Nisei Black Widow leader of a spy ring in Saturday matinee serials. He loved the sultry teasing voice of Tokyo Rose! And many more pages to suggest he never really had it at all. I may stop trying to edit or comment. Who could possibly care?

Chapter Two

May

Thank you for your patience, gentle reader. Pretty soon this narrative is going to shape into something you can make some sense of. I'm going to introduce you to a wealthy man named Nicholas Cufflett. Neither of those appellations is overtly Jewish, but he in fact has a legal claim to being Jewish. His mother was Jewish, and both grandmothers were Jewish. Nevertheless, I'm here to say the guy is not a mensch. More like a snake if I must choose a descriptive noun.

It is inconceivable to me that any Jewish mother would call her baby boy Nicholas or the name of any Christian saint, just as I could never conceive of Henry Kissinger's mother naming her son Heinrich. I question his Torah credentials.

> MMM: As if Issur Danielovitch Demsky never changed his name to Kirk Douglas. The Jewish writer Heinrich Heine was originally supposed to be named Harry, after an English friend of his father. When Jay heard that he tried to compose a standup comedy monolog with the opening line: Hello, I'm Harry Heine.

But stereotypical names or not, Cufflett is the main character here. If you question whether he is the true protagonist it will be because I had insufficient information about him to persuade you. To me he is the mover of the actions herein and all the rest of us merely observers.

I met Cufflett at a political meeting after the Jane Fonda party. This time I was dressed casually. Forget what I said about being from a more formal area of the country. I've adopted the laid back California style of attire when formality is not expressly called for. Nicholas said he grew up in Chicago. I'm from downstate on the Mississippi River, the Quad Cities. I don't think we include Chicagoans as Illini. At least I don't. Cook County could easily be a state of its own. I was in Chicago in 1968 and witnessed the anti-war demonstrations around the Democratic Convention.

How can I describe Nick? Perhaps suggesting the name of an actor that you might recognize will help create an image. He looked sort of like Jack Klugman's boss on the TV show, Quincy. He looked top management, well educated, with a confident, professional demeanor. He came to the meeting in an expensive suit and cravat and was easily the best dressed person there as I was the most casual. His hair was a style cut to flatter the shape of his head and then blown dry. Mine was the old fashioned man's haircut, wetted down with water and with a part on the left side.

He could be a year or two younger than me and he smelled nice. I don't use flagrantly fragranced deodorants in public myself. We discussed certain historical reference points about the 60s, JFK, RFK, MLK Jr. and he was definitely a contemporary of mine. Where were you when you heard---?

I've since learned that he belongs to a health club, works out regularly, has facials, manicures, and massages. We scots-irish would never think of allowing a stranger touch our naked bodies. After a certain age we don't even allow our own mothers to see us without proper strategic covering.

> MMM: In Japan massages are traditionally the domain of blind practitioners.

Re: if it were a masseur, we couldn't tolerate the homosexual overtones with strange man's hands rubbing warm oil over our backs and legs. Actually, though, I once saw an episode of I Love Lucy where John Wayne was getting a massage from a male athletic masseur. And John Wayne is scots-irish from Iowa, you know! Lucy lurking, stalking the Duke, takes over when the masseur is called away.

If it was a masseuse I could endure the sexual overtones but not the hedonistic implications of pampering myself. Come to think of it, I do like to get my haircuts at a beauty parlor with feminine hands fiddling around my head after fixing the drop cloth around my neck.

I started going to unisex hair shops when many male barbers kept smoking cigarettes as they trimmed my hair. That was awful! Unendurable! My first experience with a lady barber (a Delilah!) was in the service at the Post Exchange. From there I began to see where the ladies might enjoy the attentions of male hairdressers.

Once at an Italian eatery an attractive waitress tied a bib around my neck. I liked it. And at Pinnacle Peak steak house the waitresses put their arms around your neck to stealthily scissor off your necktie! You have to know ahead of time to wear an expendable piece of colorful cloth to that place! The severed ties hang from the ceiling like trophy scalps.

I've seen strangers hug my co-workers they never met before but they don't try to hug me. Must be something in my aura, my eyes or *je ne sais quoi* that says, don't touch. I don't know why that is. Still, I don't go for the familiar hugs of strangers that make a habit out of hugging for no reason. There should be a reason for the arms embracing other than hello there.

Nick struck me as a hedonist though he didn't flash any gold chains or pinky rings. He might be a tasteful hedonist if that concept is possible.

I didn't see his car the first time. It turned out to be a Mercedes. I was disgusted. A Jew driving a Mercedes! I'm not evenly remotely Jewish and I would never do such a thing. I supposed that it might be a disguise. Maybe he doesn't want anyone to know he's Jewish. Has a neutral name. I had the temerity later to ask him about it. He said,

"*Au contraire, mon frere.* Buying and driving a Mercedes is sticking it to the bad guys. It's saying: We're still here! And we own your cars. Yeah, yeah, yeah!"

He could say it. I didn't have to believe it.

I've lived in Los Angeles-Hollywood-Beverly Hills for years. This guy named his favorite charities and they were ones often favored by Jews, like City of Hope, and Cedars-Sinai. Then it helped that he named a relative or two who really did have Jewish names.

I've given a few dollars to the United Jewish Appeal myself over the years. Unlike some so-called liberals of my generation I'm a staunch Zionist. Liberals are supposed to be progressive but I can't find anything progressive about fanatic hate and terrorist murderers such as we saw at the Munich Olympics. Yet liberal magazines like the Nation stick up for the bad guys! Like the Middle East should be forbidden to practitioners of Judaism forever because some Grand Mufti pal of Hitler got a wild hair.

Nick and I listened to a speech at the meeting, but I saw his eyes glaze over and he didn't hear much of it. It went something like this as I recall: The PLO has been getting money, weapons and diplomatic muscle to eradicate Jewish people from anywhere near the Middle East.

The PLO announces their intention to bomb, murder, terrorize until there is no Israel. The world's reaction is to pretend this is not happening. The world prefers to pretend that there are two sides with conflicting claims over land boundaries, they are stubbornly fighting it out, and can't come to any reasonable settlement. As if! I've seen mice in snake cages also pretend there's no snake in there and no escape possible. It's denial of the obvious.

The world's solution to constant bombings and atrocities is to say to the PLO terrorists: 'Hey, calm down fellow Gentiles! You want a *judenfrei* continent? Who doesn't? You say you aren't happy with the deal you got after the war, dividing Palestine between Jews and Arabs?

Just because the French and British confiscated that part of the Ottoman Empire for backing the Kaiser, they had no right to allow Jewish refugees to return to their homeland. Why should Jews be allowed to live anywhere? Do what you have to do to correct that mistake. Just try to hold down the collateral damage to our interests in the region, huh?'

That is a just a smoke screen for insuring continued flow of petroleum into our economic profit centers. The world pretended the Holocaust was not happening either. That would be too messy to deal with. Hitler's army stood in the way.

Can there be two sides to a murderer and his victim? Try to strike a balance? That's what has happened to Liberalism. It keeps insisting everything is relative. Oh, sure, the woman tempted the rapist beyond his ability to control himself! The rich guy flaunted his gold ring in public and the mugger had to take his wallet because he'd had an impoverished childhood! Give me a break!

Two sides to every story and we must give equal weight to each side's argument. 'Now Satan, God says you were a bad son, rebellious to a fault. You got some followers to try and stage a coup against the Old Man. Convince us that your cause was necessary! We're listening with open minds!'

There should be no compromise with irrational evil! That was Ben Franklin's mistake in the formation of our constitution. The result was

Civil War and the incredibly shameful destructive poisonous segregation that we still endure a hundred years later. The idea that some folks are 3/5ths of other folks is the lie that was used to justify that peculiar institution of brutal slavery and degrading treatment by citizens who appear in the light of hindsight to have themselves been mentally deficient.

I once read a document from the pre-Lincoln presidency gagging over seeing their slaves put their hooves into dishes at the supper table. They were even denied calling their body parts by human terminology!

In the Durants Story of Civilization they cited a report from England back in the early exploration times when an ape was brought from Africa and escaped from its cage. Country folk who found it assumed its grunts were in the French language so they hung it as a spy. I had to laugh. Evidently this is the mentality that prevailed in some parts of our country before the Emancipation Proclamation and still does in too many communities.

> In this century they have a catchy marching song though:
> *Let cowards quake, while storm troops march before us*
> *We are by birth the fuhrers of the world*
> *Our leader calls and we must follow him to vic'try*
> *Great Leader calls, his banners now unfurled!*

There are a lot of refugees and many disputed territories of land in this world. The Armenians, the Azerbaijans, the Baluchis, the Basques, the Kurds, the Serbs, the Tibetans, the Seminoles, the Cherokees, the Lakota *et altera*. They don't go around blowing up airliners, shooting Olympic athletes in cold blood, or killing women and children to gain the world's admiration and support. Quisling's followers are alive and well in Norway as we see that country aiding the PLO terrorists against the Jews.

My love for the fanatic and militant barbarians campaigning to destroy both Israel and western civilization is less than my love for any other species of life on this planet.

What absolutely amazes and appalls me is the appeal from Quakers, Unitarians, and other peacemakers for food, clothing, medicine, shelter, and educational assistance to the motley group that seized the name Palestinians away from its Jewish history. The PLO has unlimited millions for munitions and warfare training camps and for staging occasional attacks on Israel and elsewhere, but no funds for food, clothing, shelters, and education for their civilian population. Oh, gosh! Pass the hat for us to feed their families!

Eventually the Armenians, the Azerbaijans, the Baluchis, the Basques, the Kurds, the Serbs, the Tibetans, the Seminoles, the Cherokees, the Lakotas and the others will find random acts of murder and terror will gain them respectability and perhaps their sovereign territory will be restored. But wait, those claimants don't have petroleum that we want, do they? Gosh, maybe I'm mistaken.

End of speech and exchanges that I heard and agreed with, blushing as a Unitarian in admitting unconscionable blinders on maybe half my fellow congregation.

As I talked with Nicholas it appeared I was even more committed to Zionism than he was. He was pulling for Shimon Peres to assume leadership in Israel. My choice was the brilliant strategist and courageous general Ariel Sharon. But then it's all academic. As if our two opinions matter a twit in the real world.

MMM: I don't know where his Zionism comes from, but he's had it all the time I've known Jay. I once asked if he thought he might be a reincarnated victim of Nazis. His answer was 'a Jew would be too forgiving, too generous, too hasty to make nice.' He said God needs Gentiles like himself to look out for His interests and His people.

There was no reason for us to become friends. Still, there was something about Nick Cufflett's smile that intrigued me. He seemed very intelligent and bemused by some of the things other people were saying. He offered a couple of whispered asides to me about the speakers that were witty and that I had to agree with. All around us folks were lighting up cigarettes. I whispered to Nick, "Are you a smoker, too?"

Nick's reply was, "Is the Pope Italian?" He pulled out a deck of fags and flashed it, then put it back in his inner suit jacket.

Then he whispered back, "Are you a non-smoker?"

I replied, "Is Stevie Nicks a girl?" This drew a delighted smile from Nick. I had tuned into his wit with repartee. It was an accident. That kind of banter is usually over my head. I'm a slow thinker, slow responder. After passionate debates I often think of a retort in the middle of the night: I should have said---

Besides the immediate political cause that brought us to the meeting we shared tastes in music, as it happened.

He asked if I'd seen the Andrew Lloyd Webber production at the Music Center. I replied, 'no, but I have the album and I also have his etc, etc.' When I asked what forms of music he admired he quoted John Cleese's famous:

"I delight in all manifestations of the terpsichorean muse."

That amused me. Cleese was in a cheese shop in a Python sketch at the time and the Muzak featured balalaikas strumming along with some sound effects of leather slapping dance floors. The only thing I dislike about watching Greek males dancing is when they throw plates and break them.

Pondering that phenomenon I came up with the concept of males flaunting their superior position over the ladies. Ha-ha! We can do anything we like. We are males. We can smash dishes and you don't dare say anything, because we are males. Dancing males. I don't remember seeing any Greek ladies dancing, shoulder to shoulder.

I mentioned several discs in my collection and Nick replied that he could match two of my treasures such as Rachmaninoff's tone poem Isle of the Dead and Paul Dukas' dance poem La Péri. I mentioned that I would like to hear Cecile Lecad, the virtuoso Filipina pianist, in concert some day. I love to see pretty ladies fiddling or playing piano. He said he had attended one of her concerts already. He one-upped me several times.

> MMM: Yes, he used that line on me before we married. I played my recital piece for him, A Maiden's Prayer by Tekla Badarzewska-Baranowska, a girl in Poland who died very young.

I don't mind being one-upped. Associating with persons with better skills advances our own skills. It's a super way to improve oneself, to be challenged by competition. In tennis you seek a better partner so you can improve your game. In chess or any other endeavor that requires practice and skill you seek a player who is more knowledgeable.

All the things that would have made me want to avoid the guy were overlooked because of some idle conversation about music and women. This particular meeting was mostly male and mostly older types. For some reason we got to talking about Mitsi and I took out my billfold to show him her picture. He was politely appreciative and then he took out his own billfold and showed me a picture of his fiancée. It was SHE!

Well, he had one-upped me again! I kept my face from reacting. I don't know what it would have done if I hadn't sent instant signals from my brain to instantly but softly freeze. Would my eyebrows have shot up? Would my mouth have gaped like a fish out of water? Would the hairs on the back of my neck crawled up? Would I have put my vocal chords in gear and shouted, "Hey! I know this girl!"

No, I just looked at it long and appreciatively and handed it back to Nick. I like to think I have poise under pressure. Maybe could have had a career in espionage. I had a flair for dramatics in high school and college and appeared in a few stage productions. I was The Sheriff in Tish, Felix Ducatel in My Three Angels and the understudy for Pooh-Bah in the Mikado.

I've already told you that SHE is a one-man girl. What I've said about that holds true. Just from that one conversation in Malibu I knew she would not be playing around on her husband. She would end it cleanly and then maybe take up with another man. She had pride, integrity, and standards of her own to live up to. This meeting with Nick was in early May just a couple of weeks after the Jane Fonda affair.

Finally I decided to say, "Hey, I'm envious as hell, man. That's a fantabulous girl!"

My face must have been the color of key lime pie. Forgive me Mitsi, my Goddess of Mercy. It was fleetingly true at the time.

MMM: I'm sure. No offense taken.

I hung my head and wondered what to say next. Didn't he know she's married? Even if she's separated, she couldn't possibly be clear of the marriage that soon. Should I say that I met her? Met her husband? I decided not to mention my meeting them.

I said, "Uh, but, uhhh, could you be robbing the cradle? Is she of the age of consent, you hound?" Inside my head I was calling him more than you hound!

He was playing it cagey. Just as he evaded any questions about where he lived or worked, or even in what line of business he came by his wealth, he dodged questions about how he came to know the lovely, incomparable SHE. He waxed poetic about her. Said she was the ultimate woman, the only woman he could ever love, and he gave the impression that he had loved a few in his time.

I tried to echo his compliments to her. I said that I was a fan of France Nuyen, Nancy Kwan, Dolores Del Rio, Elizabeth Taylor, and a few other beauties whose names escape me now. I said,

"She would even stand out in that milieu."

He agreed and upped the ante. "Her beauty is the least of her attributes."

I looked him over again, trying to guess his age. He would have to be at least twenty years older than this glorious nymph. I've found that the age barrier is put there by nature for a purpose.

I've known many, many guys who suffer a midlife crisis, marry a younger girl, and it never makes them happy. They have to work three times as hard as they did before the change -- twice for new wife's expectations and still maintain the old wife -- and I know if it was possible to put a broken egg back in the shell, most of them would try to do it. There is a generation gap in only ten years that works against a second marriage. Twenty years is just too wide a cultural gap between a man and woman.

Wives should hunker down when their mate goes into his 'last fling before hitting old age' crisis. It's a stupid phase caused by some chemical changes in the brain that men should not have to pay for with the rest of their lives. They have a tiger by the tail and need help getting loose from it. Some place of safety, if you catch my drift. Or if you want to make them pay, take them back. Either way, you extract revenge, eh?

Dick Van Dyke and Debbie Reynolds said it better than I ever could in Divorce American Style. Poor Jason Robards. Funny film.

Still, I was not going to share this advice with Nick at this time. He had shared a picture with me, and I had shared one with him. We weren't really friends, just acquaintances with a shared taste in music. I thought about SHE and her husband's band and his music. Then I said,

"Well, this lovely young girl, does she appreciate Lloyd Webber also?"

His affirmative reply included that she seemingly excelled his own knowledge in music appreciation. She knew virtuoso musicians and their respective ranks in international reputations.

She had an ear, she had perfect pitch. She had a wide range in tastes that included popular personalities of the day, as well as the older ones that we can only know from their recordings. She even had some RCA Red Label 33 rpm records with Sergei himself playing his own concertos and famous rhapsody.

Yeah, I thought. I'll bet she does. She was too good to be true. Inconceivable!

Mitsi and I love going to concerts in Los Angeles. There's the UCLA campus, of course, the Music Center downtown, Hollywood Bowl, The Los Angeles Philharmonic, The Shrine Auditorium next to USC for Michael Oistrakh. Pasadena Civic for Van Cliburn. We'd even driven out to Claremont Colleges to see Isaac Stern at their Bridges Hall. There are many smaller venues for chamber music, and Mitsi is friends with a violinist in the Sequoia Quartet. Chamber music sounds best in intimate little halls, schools, churches, or clubs at least to my way of thinking.

I've always thought the Tonight Show should feature chamber music rather than loud brassy jazz. It could set a contemplative mind clearing mood for sleep. The sponsors probably insist on brass and drum noises to keep their audience awake for their messages.

Late night talk used to have intelligent conversationalists or personalities with wit. Steve Allen and Jack Paar knew the business, created the business. Eminent guests were there to amuse with personal anecdotes, insights or experiences, to comment or demonstrate their art or skill. Dick Cavett tried to carry the torch but couldn't rally the lowest common denominators for the much more important ratings points.

Along came the corporate men in suits and ties who are so lacking in imagination and so fearful for their phony baloney jobs that they found a profitable formula that makes sponsors happy and replicated it ad nauseam. Nothing interesting is supposed to happen because it might have cause consternation with the sponsors' sensibilities!

Now every talk show is filled with predictable cheap shot, cruel barbs aimed at celebrities in the news, paid commercials and unpaid publicity for films and music albums. If you look at them, they are only infomercials with no redeeming social value. Their format allows no creativity or enlightenment, only thoughtless, witless nonsense. Lame, corporate pablum. Lame.

For the next couple of weeks, whenever Mitsi and I went out of the apartment for any reason I searched the streets, the shops, the audiences, for SHE. We never saw her, or should I say, I never saw her. Mitsi didn't know I was looking.

I surreptitiously made some phone calls, asking what band had played at the Jane Fonda fundraiser that afternoon in Malibu. It was a dead end. No one knew. No one that I knew, knew.

You'll recognize now that the scenario that I had played out on first meeting SHE was being realized by this character, Nick. He evidently had both the wherewithal and the freedom to sweep her off her feet.

I regretted never having worked hard for success. I was too easily satisfied. I'm as happy as a man in debt can be and my wife and I complement each other extremely well. Our interests mesh except for my discerning eye for beauty. I can't blame her, though. Men are not beautiful. Many of those that are, are gay, *n'est pas?*

Really, believe me, Mitsi and I make a great couple. Her culture and contacts enrich my life experiences immeasurably and no fantasy could ever detract from that reality. I recognized that the emotion I was feeling was incipient midlife crisis. Luckily I was able to control it, manage it, sublimate it, run it off into a harmless mind game.

But then it had never occurred to me that there was such a prize in this world or that I would ever meet her face to face and actually talk with her. Had I known I might have taken the trouble to collect a million dollars or two or three. But no, I'd gotten married and settled down into an easy routine of borderline bankruptcy like a lot of fellow citizens.

Nick had not been at the Jane Fonda party in April, but maybe SHE had met Nick at some other party where her husband had played drums. Maybe the scenario was perfect down to that little detail too. Maybe SHE had genes with cells that were rigged when she was a prenatal-embryo to recognize the man of her dreams when he said those magic words that would restore her to her rightful place in this world inside a palace. No other promises were necessary. Those few words were predestined to convert her into a loving, willing, perfect mate. In my case it was an accident. With Nick it could have been his standard line.

In late May I went to another political meeting and was relieved to see Nick there. SHE wasn't with him. But at least I could inquire about her. He was living my dream life, my fantasy. I wanted to know how it was going, details.

We were listening to some financial advisers and I thought I'd get a chance to wander over and pump Nick for information. When I got disentangled from the two guys I was talking with he had slipped out away from the meeting, taking French leave.

His mailing address for the meetings was a P.O. Box in Brentwood and his phone number was unlisted. He had my business card so there was a chance he might phone me some day if we didn't meet up again. I was devastated that he had disappeared. I didn't want to live another month without knowing what was happening to my alter ego with SHE.

Years ago I had a similar obsession with Emma Peel. You remember, Diana Rigg, from the Avengers. John Steed was my alter ego in that one. Steed, Patrick Macnee, now lives in Beverly Hills, I think. Haven't seen him around. I suppose he wouldn't be attired in Edwardian apparel with a bowler so therefore has a lower profile.

Anyway I read in the Times several years ago that Diana was appearing in London on the stage in full frontal nudity. I knuckled my eyes in disbelief and read the news article again. A dream come true? It could not happen!

All I would have to do is scare up some round trip airfare, make up a story for Mitsi for flying off for a few days, and I could enjoy seeing this fabulous actress as God made her, in the actual flesh. It could not happen!

I procrastinated around, as usual. The play was a hit of course and had a good run in London. Eventually I assumed it had passed me by. It was just one of those ephemeral golden opportunities that tantalize us and then dissolve when the sun goes down.

But oh-no no-oh! Next I read in the Times that they were taking the play on tour. They were taking it to Los Angeles! Diana Rigg was going to appear nude at the Ahmanson! Unbelievable! I must be God's favorite this year. Unbelievable!

Still there was some hesitation in my joy. The city fathers were a pretty uptight bunch of bluenoses who routinely gave fine art exhibits a rough time. Surely they would not stand for this play being presented in the cultural center of the city, practically across the street from City Hall. Maybe the producers would cut the scene to satisfy our provincial censors.

The play was Abelard and Heloise with a religious-sacrilegious theme. How could such inflammatory stuff play in the City of Angels? But the day came and no riot squad turned out to arrest the actors. I was destined to see it. I was almost obliged to buy a ticket.

I went to the Ahmanson the second night it opened and waited in the cancellations line for one good seat. Amazingly they had one in the center about the fifth row. I must have died and gone to heaven. What had I ever done to deserve this incredible fantasy made flesh? A naked Diana Rigg served up to my eyes on a platter.

If you saw it, you know that at the end of the second act, Abelard and Heloise come out from separate sides of the stage, nude, and run quickly into an embrace, and then a blackout. Well, I wasn't quick enough. The program had not said at what point Diana Rigg would emerge from stage wings, nude, for the briefest hug ever presented before an audience. Two to three seconds at most.

I barely remember the quick embrace and seeing nude thighs and then lights out. Huh? That was it? I had blinked evidently. I could always say I was there for the event but hadn't been allowed to truly savor it. Well, that's the way life is. I was thankful for the crumb.

Life is a whole lot more satisfying when you lower your expectations and go along with the pageant that takes place around you and outside of your ability to influence. Everybody gets a thrill once in awhile. I attended one of the performances of Hair! at the Aquarius Theater in Hollywood, owned at the time by Tommy Smothers and his manager

Ken Kragen. In the famous nude scene there were shadows that pretty well hid what had been advertised. That was OK, too. I didn't really want to see the guys, and with the shadows on the girls there was nothing to see.

> MMM: I didn't know about Abelard and Heloise but I was with him at Hair! I don't think the producers spent a dime on costumes for Hair! Good music, though.

Chapter Three

June

By the second week in June, Mitsi was on summer hiatus at the university. She took off with her sister for a trip to New Zealand. They would be doing some skiing since June is winter down under. I drove Mitsi, her sister and their luggage to the airport, Los Angeles International (LAX).

While waiting at the gate for them to board I killed some time browsing the art paintings for sale at a boutique in the Tom Bradley International Terminal. Most of the paintings were Los Angeles area scenes, sort of like giant, oil painted postcards: Orange groves, Hollywood Bowl, Chinatown, Olvera Street, Santa Monica Pier, Long Beach, Movie Studios. A few were portrait style paintings of John Wayne, Marilyn Monroe, James Dean and other iconic actors but their likenesses were not as photo-realistic as portraits by Norman Rockwell.

After I entered the shop I spotted an alcove not visible from the outside. There was a four by six foot painting of a reclining nude that was partially blocked for viewing by minors. It was extremely realistic so I assumed it was a photo transferred to canvas to make it appear like a painting by Caravaggio or Titian. The manager of the shop was busy so I couldn't ask about it or inquire the price.

After my wife and her sister boarded the plane I went back to see and price the nude painting. It was gone. It had been sold in that brief period of time before I got a good look at it. That happens to me a lot. I'm often just in time to be too late.

Getting into the elevator to return to the parking lot there was a prosperous looking older man with a pre-teen girl getting off. I stood aside and noticed the girl was carrying a buggy whip, and was expensively dressed in some kind of riding outfit with boots. I sucked on one side of my cheek the way Harvey Korman does in those TV sketches and said softly,

"Hmmm, kinky."

It was an impure thought. She was probably his granddaughter and they en route to a horse show. If you didn't understand why I said kinky maybe you haven't read Nabokov's Lolita. It's a neglected masterpiece because people are afraid of the subject matter. Two mature men, Humbert Humbert and Clare Quilty, obsess over the favors of a prepubescent girl. One of them gets sidetracked and seeks revenge with a gun.

I'm a fearless reader. Nothing is too far out for me anymore. Stephen Hawking is a little beyond my reach, but that doesn't mean I won't try to read and understand some of it. James Michener's books have impressed me with his scenarios all over the world and all over the centuries. I've read them all until his most recent one.

If you remain at the Los Angeles Airport terminal long enough you will see everyone you've ever known or ever hoped to meet. They all pass through those gates eventually. You may notice that I borrowed that observation from descriptions of the New York Times Square location. I'm great at recycling ideas as well as resources.

On the sidewalk across from the parking lot on that Saturday afternoon I saw a familiar head of hair ahead of me. I overtook her and sure enough it was SHE. She was carrying an overnight case, one she'd obviously tucked under the seat of the plane. Two pickup artists were hitting on her and begging to carry the little bag for her. She shook her head no and turned away from them.

I walked up beside her and said, "Hello, may I carry that bag for you?"

Luckily for my ego she recognized me. She shook a 'no' to the bag carrying part but gave me a cheerful, 'Hello, nice to see you again.' The two young punks took off. I didn't even have to make any faces at them.

This seemed a great opportunity for extracting information, the answer to my prayers. I said "Isn't your husband here to meet the plane?"

She answered, "No, he's out of town on a job. I'm taking a taxi home."

To myself I thought what a fool this guy is. He allows her to take a taxi. Or maybe even catch a ride with a predatory or perverted stranger. That fellow must not be too bright. What could he have been thinking, sending his wife home alone? Didn't he have some support group that was supposed to meet her plane and watch over her? Or, on the other hand maybe she had she been out of town on a tryst with Nick while her husband was out of town.

"Oh, please," I said, hoping my voice didn't have too much begging in it. "Please let me drive you home. I was just here seeing my sister off on the plane so her car is close by in the short term parking lot."

That was partially true. My sister-in-law was traveling with my wife. It scares me sometimes how easily lies could fall off my tongue without passing my brain at all. Somehow I had recycled the prepared excuse for the Volvo that wasn't used at the Malibu fundraiser. It was my sister's car. Amazing, this newly discovered subconscious or automatic talent for prevarication.

I told her my sister left her station wagon in my care and again suggested that it would be easier for her to ride with me than with a taxi, although the logic in that argument eludes me even today.

She thought about it for a moment. Then she smiled and said, "OK."

I knew it! She would have gone with me from the party if I'd put the question to her back in April. She's unable to say 'no' to me. Those magic words: Let me buy you this palace. I'm one of the few mortals she's been programmed to respond to.

She had no luggage to pick up at the carousel. She'd been out of town with just the overnight case. Dare I ask if it was possibly with Nick Cufflett, our possibly mutual friend? Would he be foolish enough to let her travel alone? Maybe had business to take care of? We would have plenty of time in the car so I held back those questions for the moment.

As we crossed the street to the parking lot I asked her, "Do you like Volvos?"

She answered, "I haven't been in many cars in America. We only have the van and my husband drives it. I don't know how to drive."

I unlocked the passenger door and held it while she put her overnight case on the floorboards and then got into the car. It occurred to me suddenly that I had not opened the car door for my wife for years. I made a mental note that I needed to go back to opening doors for her again.

> MMM: He's forgotten that we had a talk and I told him I am a career woman, not helpless or dependent. I don't require or expect him to open the door for me.

So she was sticking to that husband story, intimating they were still man and wife. I have the kind of mind that needs to sort out details and make some sense of them.

"I hope I'm not out of line, prying too much. But, do you enjoy following your husband around on his jobs?"

She said, "At first I did, but we've been married five months now and I think it's a waste of time and boring to hear the same tunes over and over. Parties are not special when you attend them every weekend and sometimes twice on Saturday."

There is an explanation as to how she uses such perfect English in these pages. I can't remember exactly her accent and therefore have not tried to recreate her dialog with broken English. Sorry if it distracts you from the authenticity.

The rest of her story made sense. Her husband had driven the van up to the San Francisco area where his brother also has a band and a lot of June bookings for dances, weddings, and graduation parties. SHE had gone along only to meet the brother and his family.

Her husband would continue to play at jobs for the rest of the month up there; she was to return to their apartment where she would study her English with workbooks and tape recorded lessons. There was no room for her at the brother's place, although presumably they could have put sleeping bags in the van.

Husband put her on a plane in Oakland and gave her cab fare home with two weeks grocery allowance. Said he'd send more if she needed it. He let this treasure run loose! Remember how I doubted his intelligence back there at the party?

I hesitated a moment and then queried, "Ever hear of a man named Nick Cufflett?"

She answered, "Yes, he booked my husband's band at that party where I met you. He's booked several jobs for my husband, has a lot of contacts around town."

"He's a talent agent?"

"No, he's a millionaire that just does favors for people. He doesn't get any money for it. He doesn't need it."

Well that explained a lot. Cufflett has eyes for her, but hasn't made his move yet. Fiancée was a premature word. He's eating his heart out right now the same as I am. Poor puppy.

I asked her how well she knew Nick, because I knew him by reputation, as if that logic allowed me to pry. She said she didn't know him at all. That he hung out with her husband and the band sometimes, but she hadn't really talked much with Mr. Cufflett. Mr. Cufflett! Ha! She has a version and he has a version. Anyone would take her word against the blow-dried Mr. Cufflett. She may be his intended bride, but she didn't know it.

I dug the hole I was digging even deeper then. I asked her,

"Aren't you afraid to stay alone at your apartment, without your husband there to protect you?"

She admitted she was afraid. Their place was in a rough neighborhood, and there were always young men on the street that gave her a hard time. She said she mostly stayed inside, with the door double-locked, with a baseball bat for protection.

"So, you're going to be barricaded for two weeks. That stinks! You didn't come to this country to be a prisoner inside a small apartment." My mind called up a recent song by Tom Petty and the Heartbreakers called, 'You Don't Have to Live Like a Refugee!'

She replied that she could not barricade herself for those two weeks because she had a job. She only went on band gigs with her husband on Fridays, Saturdays, and Sundays. She said she took a bus to a sewing factory five days a week. I was stunned. I could not imagine her in a sweatshop. I didn't know there were any left, had the impression that all garments are imported from overseas sweatshops these days. Is it possible that some frocks at Saks Fifth Avenue don't have Made in Bangladesh or Thai labels in them?

She talked about writing letters to her family, saying that America was wonderful, and she didn't have to tell me she was lying in those letters. Then she did something that altered the course of my life forever. She burst into tears. I should have put my arms around her or opened the glove box to a supply of Kleenex but I was driving and she had turned away toward the passenger door. She wasn't looking for comfort from me.

I didn't know what to do. Would it be out of line for me to stick my nose in and offer some advice? Probably. I carefully, pointedly, steered clear of telling her that Nicholas Cufflett, a man of means that she had already met, would soon make a move on her. For all I knew the bit with her picture was just a joke he was playing on me.

Then she said, "My marriage was a mistake. I was a dummy. I should never have married even to come to America."

I'm a sucker for the helpless damsel in distress. I used to read about the Knights of the Round Table and all that chivalry code of conduct. In the marines I never got a chance to save any villagers from the bad guys. I just learned how to duck walk up the side of a mountain with my rifle across my shoulders and imbecilic nonsense like that. I prefer to believe that I have no citations for conspicuous gallantry mainly due to lack of opportunity.

My first thought was, 'Hey, give her your apartment for two weeks and then you stay at your brother's.' But you just don't do that. No matter how pure your intentions that is just not done even for an angel in distress. First of all she'd think it was a pass. Second of all, maybe it would be. And third of all, what about Mitsi's clothes?

MMM: Yes, what about them?

So now what do I do? Drop her at her apartment and forget about her? She and her husband have a life, such as it is. She's got a job, and he's working, more or less, and they just might make it.

She described the location of her apartment and the buses she took to work. Both were on the southeast side of L.A. She couldn't get to her job without passing through the dregs of humanity downtown Los Angeles. If she was to continue to work the next two weeks, she'd have to go back to her apartment near a bus stop that took her to the sweat shop.

MMM: By 'dregs of humanity' my husband did not mean the poor. He finds nobility in the poor. He meant only the drunks and street hustlers who gravitate to the less well policed parts of the city.

What if she were to stay with a female relative of mine in Santa Monica for those two weeks until her husband returns? I didn't have a sister nearby to introduce her to, but I did have a cousin of the female persuasion, that had a two bedroom apartment in Santa Monica. For several years she had lived with a young man named Peter something but recently he had returned to his native New Zealand after taking training as a deep sea diver here in town. San Pedro, I presumed.

My cousin's name is Susan. You might picture her as Sigourney Weaver; I do. She's still in her twenties, sort of tall but very attractive, just never found a suitable husband. Susan has impossible standards. I tried to fix her up a few times but she always found fault with them.

Susan had her fling at passionate love with that Peter fellow from Kiwi Land. Now she wanted the old money type for security. Yuppies were not good enough. She made fun of them. She wanted a comfortable, well to do, and laid back man for sharing the good life, not someone working hard for more money. Not many of those around, at least in my circles.

Susan has a science teaching credential, teaches English to foreigners -- we have a lot of them -- and also is an aspiring screenwriter. Of course in our neighborhood, that is redundant, eh? Who doesn't have a script to sell? Even I do. In fact I have two completed scripts and several treatments.

Partially to console herself when her relationship with Peter was broken, she delved into a best selling book by a teacher and Unitarian minister called 'Everything I Needed to Know, I Learned in Kindergarten' or something like that. After enjoying Robert Fulghum's essays and insights she decided to deconstruct the book word by word. She typed it into her desk Mac using Excel for each word. After it was all typed in, she pressed a button to alphabetize the words.

With this long word list she went through and pruned it of all the duplications and plurals. She wasn't interested in how many times the word 'the' was used. That was old analysis. She wanted to find out how many different English words were needed to produce this volume of comment about our history and culture. It turned out that Fulghum used just over 3,000 different words.

She could not pin it down precisely because there were some words he used that seemed to be his own private jargon. For example what we might call a 'jalopy' he calls a 'hoopy'. Where we might say 'yuletide' or 'Christmas time' he writes 'Christmastide.' Other words were just obscure names and places.

Susan said this kind of analysis is used by scholars to create for example, a Shakespeare Dictionary, a volume with only words from his plays with meanings as he might have defined them, not the meanings we impart to them today. There are other specialized word list/dictionaries such as: The Baseball Dictionary, the New York Times 1976 Editions Dictionary, every word used in section one of that daily newspaper for a year. A Los Angeles Times Comics Page Dictionary, with all the words used on its comics pages for a defined period of time. Maybe the first of all these analytical dictionaries was the Holy Bible Dictionary. That must have needed a large team of data entry people.

She thought her word list/definitions within the context of that one comprehensive book could be called THE EVERY WORD I NEED TO KNOW DICTIONARY for ESL students. In her experience many of them wasted a lot of time learning English words from their dictionaries that are never used much anymore in the real world.

But here is the unintended insight Susan came up with. All those words from that best seller, with her definitions for each word, in the context of that one book according to her best knowledge, was on a disc that might cost less than $1. In fact that $1 disc could hold dozens of books. This could bring meaningful differences regarding paper vs. electronic discs and issues involving storage vs. library shelves, saving the forests, and revolutionizing the information market.

Although therapeutic, the activity had not returned any pecuniary rewards so she occasionally took in foreign students from the nearby colleges and universities to help pay the rent at a very upscale apartment house in a very convenient location.

Susan had a little side business gilding Hawaiian maile leaves to make pendant jewelry. I believe she uses 24 carat gold and that it takes some skill to apply to the leaf without destroying it. The appeal of such doodads escapes me, but I don't claim to be the average citizen. You need such a side business when you are living on a teacher's salary and depending on sales of your writing.

With any luck, SHE could be introduced as a foreign student, and not a homeless refugee. Susan knew me, though. She knew me and Mitsi. There was no chance I could make it sound innocent.

Well, doggone it, it was innocent! And just to prove it to myself I confessed the true story and SHE then knew I was married, and even though living in Beverly Hills I was hopelessly in debt from living beyond my means. I told her I felt very paternalistic toward her and would like to help her get her life organized within the limits of my resources.

She listened to my story without comment. At first I wondered if I had made a complete fool of myself. As if she had ever even considered me for potential romance or husband material. I didn't refer to that line I had told at the Jane Fonda party. I just laid out my situation for her under the guise of offering fatherly but limited help. She nodded and made no reply, as if she wasn't really listening or hadn't been expecting anything anyway.

I'm glad I got it off my chest. Now there would be no misunderstandings and my conscience was clean with Mitsi. I wasn't doing anything that any other upright decent American citizen wouldn't do for a young lady in need of assistance.

I blurted out my suggestion she take a break from their apartment and her job and stay with my cousin Susan for two weeks in Santa Monica. "You could even practice your English with her. She's a teacher."

She kept apologizing for her English, but it was not necessary. She said that back home she always felt out of place. Her parents had many social obligations and her father was away a lot of the time as an architect. She was a middle child and may have noticed that the first child and youngest child seemed to have preordained niches in families.

She had hoped that the drum player's home was her rightful place, but it wasn't. She met him when he toured on a contract over there with a band. He seemed wonderful at the time where there were no illegal recreational drugs in her home town, but here in America, all his earnings went for marijuana.

Their South Gate apartment had no furnishings to speak of, not even a bed, but back home she had also slept on the floor. He refused to teach her to drive. He wanted her to stay home all the time and party with him and his friends. Parties with marijuana and dissonant music were not the answer to her dreams, though. She only wanted to find out why she felt out of place, to find where she belonged, to go there and be happy.

It wasn't much to ask for. I stopped at a pay phone in a gas station to call Cousin Susan. She said, 'Sure, sounds interesting.' Susan is a people person and could take two weeks of almost anyone just for the novelty. She said she'd take in the young refugee for the two weeks. We drove by her place so SHE could see the Santa Monica area I had in mind. SHE seemed impressed and thought the neighborhood was a quantum leap from her husband's digs.

We then took the 10 Freeway followed by the 710 Freeway to her apartment and picked up most of her books, clothes and notions. Is that the right word for brushes, shampoos, hairpins and stuff? I didn't go inside with her. It seemed like trespassing on some guy's turf already without actually going into his home. And she didn't want me to go in. She might have been ashamed of it.

SHE needed to understand the necessity of not giving her husband Susan's phone number or address because that could cause Susan lots of trouble. SHE understood. She said she'd call him sometimes but not give any indication of where she was staying.

As for the job, I told her to call in sick for two weeks; that I would put up the wages she would have earned, while we sorted out just what she wanted to do or what options she had. I was convinced that her fluency in English was sufficient, and that she was personable enough to find a position outside of the sweat shops, perhaps in a travel agency, or a receptionist somewhere.

I had to sell her on the idea that Los Angeles is spread out over a wide area and lacks decent public transportation. It was designed to require all citizens to have their own automobiles. She must learn to drive if she is to be getting around at all outside of an apartment. She said she begged her husband to teach her to drive the van and he kept ignoring her. Actually, I must admit that was a smart move on his part. He should want to keep her home and inside.

Given a choice of teaching driving or defusing a ticking bomb, I would opt for the bomb every time. I taught Mitsuko and I find it hard to believe I'm still alive. One of us must have guardian angels that used up a lot of credits with Heaven to get us through that ordeal.

> MMM: Jay was white as a sheet before I even pulled away from the curb. That's probably why the car jumped the curb on the other side of the street. After a few lessons we decided I should enroll in a formal drivers training school with dual controls.

I offered to begin the process of getting a driver's license and some behind the wheel experience.

I also repeated again that since Susan is a teacher she could probably find her a job as a teacher's aide that paid minimum wage, which was about what the sweatshop with piece work was netting her anyway. SHE seemed grateful for my offer and for my paternal attitude. She said she needed someone like me to guide her. She said, thank you many times with bow gestures.

As we were driving back toward Susan's condo with her things I said,

"Are you familiar with Andrew Lloyd Webber's music?"

She answered, "Oh, yes. My family back home has a record store. That's where I met my husband. His band did some publicity with the shop and he kept coming back to see me all those months his tour contract kept him over there."

So Cufflett did know something about her after all. He knew of her familiarity with popular recording artists and the music world in general. Of course he could have gotten that information at second hand from talking with her husband.

I said, "How is it that you speak English so well?"

She answered, "I don't speak it well. But it was my favorite subject in school. In middle school we had an American English teacher and I was in love with him. I tried to be his favorite student. I studied hard." She blushed at the remembrance of the American teacher and her teenage crush. That teacher had a nickname for her -- Capricious Girl.

When we got to Susan's apartment we unloaded the station wagon in three trips. Susan was in the swimming pool and wasn't much help. It was a warm day. After carrying the stuff upstairs I could use a swim but didn't want to drive all the way home for a suit. I was in the market for a new one anyway.

I suggested we go a couple of blocks downtown and buy a couple of serviceable if not stylish swim suits. She had no objection and we found a department store with a small selection. I picked up some khaki trunks and she selected a white one piece suit that was only twenty dollars.

I got my money's worth on the suit. Back at Susan's when she came out of the bedroom in the swim suit it was practically see-through. What has become of swim suit manufacturers anymore? Have they no shame? Don't they make opaque material or heavy linings anymore? Her nipples showed clearly through the garment! But she seemed oblivious. These days girls are something!

I hoped she hadn't noticed my staring. At the time I could only offer a prayer to the Almighty: Thank you, Lord God, thank you, thank you, thank you, Master Artist and Creator for your blessings on mankind.

We went to the pool and she enjoyed some dog paddling around. She had piled her hair on top of her head and pinned it, and tried to keep her head and hair above water while splashing around in the pool.

The apartment complex owner, Tom Nishinaka, was there. SHE was introduced to him by Susan and I could see from his eyes that he was immediately enchanted. Susan told me privately that he's a divorced man with a bad habit of going down to Gardena every Friday and Saturday night for poker games.

Susan said Tom had been born in an internment camp in Idaho during the war. He had a rock and gem stone collection that was fabulous. Susan said Tom's father had started the collection during that compulsory wilderness sojourn in the 40s.

For many years the Nishinaka clan had raised strawberries on the Westside and tended the yards of well to do families in Santa Monica and Beverly Hills. Tom inherited some land and put up some very nicely landscaped apartments he named Sakura Gardens which is where Susan now lived.

The cash flow from the units was enough for his needs. He no longer worked his gardening route, but kept a hand in by landscaping the complex, and helping out friends who were still in the gardening business. You might call him semi-retired. Susan told me later that his ex-wife was a *haku-jin*.

SHE received a sincere welcome from Tom. His eyes were big around. SHE got his full attention while the introductions and chit-chat got started. How can I describe Tom? He was almost as tall as Susan, 5' 9" at least. He worked outdoors a lot so he was tan.

If you are familiar with the film Flower Drum Song he looked a lot like James Shigeta. Shigeta once played a Chinese railroad worker who sheds his queue, studies quick draw gun fighting and then walked like a dragon in a movie titled Walk Like a Dragon. I loved it. I think Mel Torme was in it as a gunfighter also. The beautiful young Nobu McCarthy was the love interest. She played a Chinese girl in the California gold fields that needed protection.

Tom asked me some questions when we had some privacy. I filled him in on her background as far as I knew it, even to the extent of warning him about the possibility of her husband taking umbrage and kicking on the apartment gate some time.

Tom didn't flinch. I suppose his immersion in the gambling world had toughened him up emotionally. He said something I didn't quite catch, but it was something like, 'Don't worry, I handle security around here.'

When I was satisfied that SHE and Susan would be getting along together I took my leave to let them get organized. I drove back to my digs on Bedford Drive, parked the Volvo in the underground garage with a dozen other cars and took the elevator up to good old number 401.

All the apartment houses on the street seemed to have a four story limit, some sort of zoning thing. Numbers 401, 402, 403, and 404 were all what we call penthouses. No roof top gardens but top story views with no one tap dancing or bouncing a basketball over your ceiling. Number 401 has a nice north view of Bedford Drive and what passes for an urban forest of green and shade.

I checked the mail, just some bills and solicitations of donations for worthy causes. Mitsi says I'm on everyone's sucker list. I took a shower to get rid of the chlorine smell on my body from Susan's pool. Turned on the TV but didn't really pay much attention to it. Just went into a stupor zone and fell asleep on the couch. Around 1 AM I got up, turned off the TV and went to bed.

The next morning I phoned Susan to see if SHE wanted to take a driving lesson. Susan indicated yes, they had already finished eating breakfast; it would be a nice day for a drive. Susan can drive but doesn't have a car. You must have one if you live here, but there's always one or two exceptions.

In her case, the school where she teaches is near her apartment. Santa Monica is one of Los Angeles's full service suburbs. Plenty of shops, supermarkets, and restaurants and they are not spread out like the other cities. If they don't have it, you don't need it.

The Big Blue Bus can whisk you north or south on Lincoln, or east on Wilshire. As long as where you want to go is on Wilshire or Lincoln, the bus will stop for you up every fifteen minutes. Like Sunset Boulevard, Wilshire ends at the ocean where the sun goes down so you can forget about going very far west on it.

Therefore at 10 AM I was ringing the bell at Susan's number 306. SHE came out in a nice summer cotton dress and we drove over to the DMV on Colorado and Cloverfield. I assisted her on the application form for a learner's permit, and we went ahead and got her a California ID card also. Never hurts to have good photo ID, especially if you are a foreigner. We picked up a booklet so she could study our traffic laws in her native tongue. California is very accommodating to citizens with English as a Second Language.

Back at Tom's apartment complex Susan was packing a picnic lunch for us. She was wearing a T-shirt that said: A woman without a man is like a pizza without anchovies. Later, when Susan was not close by, SHE asked me what that meant. I found it hard to explain. Shrugged an I dunno.

The three of us drove up the coast highway to Malibu and found a spot to unload a beach umbrella and some folding canvas chairs. None of us were talkative there. The wind and the surf were competition for the sound of voices. Susan brought wide straw hats and sunglasses for her and SHE.

Dining outdoors adds flavor to a meal. The simplest white bread with Oscar Mayer Bologna (product placement pending) and French's Yellow Mustard is a banquet for me *alfresco*. Adding to the flavor is that it was prepared by someone else and it is free. It tastes indescribably better than anything I could prepare for myself.

> MMM: Jay used to be partial to Vienna Sausage mini-sandwiches until they switched to chicken.

Susan had a canvas bag with varieties of Snapple to wash the sandwiches down. I selected an apple juice and a bag of Fritos to complete my snack. After watching the beach scene and some volleyball players for an hour we packed up and prepared to drive back to the apartment.

It was a week day so there weren't many cars in the parking lot. SHE started the engine and put it in neutral and got a feel for how the accelerator responds. When she got comfortable with the sound of the running motor, she put it in gear and eased the vehicle into motion. If the car got away from her the sand all around the parking lot would slow her down until I could turn off the ignition. She circled the asphalt area, coasted into a parking slot, and turned off the motor. It was an easy first step.

I went around the car and got into the drivers seat and we drove by the estate where Jane Fonda had been the catalyst for our first meeting. Susan seemed to know a little bit about the people who owned it. She gets the local newspapers. Susan regretted not attending that garden party and blamed me for not personally insisting she come.

On the spur of the moment we found another beach parking lot with no parked cars and SHE got behind the steering wheel and started the motor, put it in gear and drove around the barriers, just to refresh her earlier lesson. She was easy on the gas and heavy on the brakes, which is the way I like it in driving students. After a dozen circles of the lot she wanted a rest, so I took over and drove along the coast keeping an eye out for another likely place to practice. There were two more good spots for practice and she improved each time. Quick learner. Four lessons in one day!

MMM: Huuuummmff!

It was still early and we impulsively kept on going north on Pacific Coast Highway all the way toward Santa Barbara, just past Oxnard and Carpenteria. There is a beach resort just south of the Santa Barbara city limits called the Miramar Inn where Mitsi and I like to stay overnight in bungalows on the sand and surf. The breakers lull us to sleep and we wake to their unique sound in the morning. The Inn has a restaurant with great sea scallops according to Mitsi. I prefer a filet mignon with baked potato for supper.

Our party of three had an early supper at the Inn. The beach snack had not been substantial enough. I had to fight Susan for the check. She thought my contribution of the car and gasoline had been sufficient.

As we drove back toward Santa Monica SHE asked Susan what she taught. Susan said she was a science specialist at a private elementary and middle school. For example, she had just prepared an explanation about the origins of the universe for her seventh and eighth graders. She mentioned the theory that all the stars, planets, quasars, black holes, etc. are currently in an expanding universe but eventually, like a rubber band, all of the matter in the universe would stop expanding and then snap back towards the point where the Big Bang originally exploded.

Possibly the Bang Explosion and the Predicted Implosion are continuing pulse beats, repeating the action. According to one theory, during the journey backwards, time may reverse itself.

"That's as much as I tell the kids because that's about as much as we can ask them to digest at their age," Susan said.

She continued, "I don't tell them that some scientists believe that during the implosion stage there's a possibility of time reversal when the dead will rise from their graves, be restored to life and health and keep getting younger. People will relive every moment of their lives backwards, meeting everyone they ever knew. When they have grown smaller and are babies again, they will enter their mother's womb, thus never seeing death on the backwards journey."

Susan and I have had this conversation before, so she seemed to be soliciting my comment on this sort of bizarre theory. I said,

"Yeah, I have given it some thought. Resurrection and eternal life as long as the universe pulses in and out. Life is superior to matter, so it must endure if matter endures. It is science's answer to our concepts of eternal life, isn't it?"

Susan replied, "It may even include a Protestant concept of predestination."

"And might explain déjà vu," SHE added. As I said earlier, this kid has a mind that works. "And it sounds a lot like the Taoist Yin and Yang, too."

Susan continued, "It is compatible with Buddhism and Hinduism with its many incarnations on a journey to Oblivion. Heaven or Hell would not be in another dimension but a return to this dimension for sequential bodies over the thousands of years of mankind. I think we might even include the Jehovah's Witnesses in this scenario. It's a pretty large umbrella. The Catholic ideas of serving time in limbo and purgatory could fit nicely into the multiple incarnations as well."

"As a young boy," I said, "I once read Ripley's Believe It or Not describing the size of Heaven in earthly measuring units as stated in the Book of Revelations. Ripley said, 'You want to be with your parents, and your parents want to be with their parents, and their parents want to be with their parents. If you are planning to meet your family members again there's going to be a terribly awkward crush of souls in circles within circles and it won't be easy to find the ones you want. You're going to have a Hell of a time in Heaven.'

"There you go," Susan said. "Maybe Heaven is strung out over millions of years so we only meet our parents, our children and our spouses and friends on one of the pulses and pursue other activities or families in subsequent pulses depending on our life programs. Then we could discard the idea of unearned paradise or an earned hell. We progress across thousands of lifetimes. At the end of infinite incarnations we find Eternal Life or Oblivion.

Orrrrr, maybe Oblivion is only the period before the Explosion and Life again. It seems a neater theory if the only universal law is that change is the only constant. Could Christians and Buddhists both be right?

Two twin sisters arguing: Certs is a breath mint! Certs is a candy mint! Certs is a breath mint! Certs is a candy mint! Stop! You are both right! Certs is two mints in one!

And if you analyze it, there is no waiting in the grave for the reanimation. Time does not exist where the human psyche does not exist. Time is an invention we came up with to plant crops, to count heavenly body rotations, and to keep appointments. Clocks were invented so monks would all pray at the appointed time together."

SHE contributed, "Einstein said time is what keeps everything from happening at once."

That startled me for a moment. I'll have to digest that and insert it in my 'time does not exist where human psyche does not exist' thought. I haven't fully absorbed any of this esoteric stuff. It's just that I'm willing to withhold critical judgment and pursue a line to see where it's going.

I commented, "Even after we try to use science to explain a mystery, it still remains a mystery, doesn't it?"

Inside my head I conjured up a picture of those blind sages touching an elephant at various parts of its body, then describing the elephant as a tree, a wall, a snake, based on their limited experience with one aspect.

Then we agreed to file those thoughts into the back of our minds for pondering when our critical responses wouldn't interfere. In my own head I could fit it into Unitarians, where I've studied the transcendental philosophy and contributed to its proliferation, but I've never outright rejected the Presbyterians that I was born into. There isn't any conflict with Christianity so far as I can see in the original concept. There may be doctrinal deviations developed by Paul, Augustine, and Aquinas but the universal picture may be larger than any human mind had the scope to embrace in the last 3,000 years.

When I saw that giant storage warehouse at the end of Raiders of the Lost Ark I imagined a gnat emerging from a discarded sprig of grapes from a storage worker's lunch. The gnat looks around and says to another gnat: "We seem to be alone in the universe. At least there's no sign of life anywhere but on our sprig of grapes. We must appear to be gods to those micro-organisms we see on each other's body! We must be the dominant life form in the universe! I wonder what our purpose is? How did we come to be and what will happen to this universe warehouse if we become extinct?"

With our short lives, our limited vision, our pitiful tools, but tremendous egos atheists imagine humanity is the center of the universe, and then have the temerity to say they've looked around and there is no *raison d'etre*, because there is no god, just us! It must take a gnat-sized brain to claim to have that omniscience.

> MMM: Jay never mentioned that theory to me. He said more than once that I intimidated him with my intellect and he didn't want to expose his lack of intelligence for fear of losing my respect for him. I'm not going to comment on it. My family is Buddhist and Shinto. We are transcendentalist and feel harmony with the universe however it works. It is not a topic for debate or speculation in our culture.

As we said our good nights back at their apartment SHE said she would enjoy taking that same drive on Route One to practice for her driver's license again. That part of the coast can be seen more than once. You have to pay close attention to steering because the road winds around and up and down. I like to save the part about parallel parking until a person has more of a feel for the car and for where the four corners of it are when it is moving.

When I phoned Susan the next day she said Tom wanted to take them out with an eye to being a driving instructor also. It suited me. Like me, he also invited Susan along as a chaperone.

I spoke to Susan again later in the week. It seems Tom donated his old Maxima station wagon so SHE and Susan could use it in perpetuity as long as they live in his apartment building. He acquired a brand new more impressive vehicle for himself, a Chrysler Town and Country. I had to smile when I realized that even for an upgraded image he went for utility and proven drive trains. Tom and I were both pragmatists.

This made it easier so SHE could practice because Susan already had a driver's license and could accompany her with trips to the market and shopping. A week later I was invited to go along on a repeat of that drive up the coast to Santa Barbara. I rode shotgun and SHE and Susan traded off from time to time.

SHE was told that the passenger sitting to the right of the driver takes the most risk in case of an accident. Sometimes it is referred to as the Suicide Seat, but teenage boys like to call it Shotgun. At least boys in my day called it that, as if they were riding on a stagecoach in the old cowboy days, assisting the driver by keeping lookout for highwaymen's guns or hostile natives bows and arrows. The part about the suicide seat was to impress upon her the concept of seat belt protection.

On this trip our heavy conversation was centered on my anger at the worst criminal of the twentieth century who has actually become a folk hero. This is the way I framed my challenge to Susan: Name the idiot who messed up the world for the rest of us and has never been called to account.

I wanted to impress both the young ladies with my keen analytical ability to challenge the media blitz of information that seems to control our perceptions of the world.

Susan gave the usual responses about political leaders and war makers and seemed surprised when I told her that in my opinion it was someone known to the world as D. B. Cooper. If he had never been born millions of people would be much better off today.

He is the fellow whose parents were probably not married, who popularized airplane hijacking. He came up with the concept of bringing a gun onto a plane, and using the passengers as hostages for the delivery of a large sum of money and the airliner for escape. He was rewarded with a modest fortune, and he bailed out of the plane over a largely unpopulated area, and has never been found, presumed dead. Sure, that's what they want us to believe!

Since his success and the authorities cravenly acquiescing to copycat criminal demands, the airlines failing to do anything reasonable to prevent further hijackings, it led to an epidemic of hostage based extortion.

Rewarding criminals to save hostages is the exact opposite of what should be our policy. To some extent I first noticed this counterproductive policy when it began with LAPD officers in The Onion Field, described by Joseph Wambaugh, a one time Los Angeles police officer, now an author.

Two criminals took on two police officers. One criminal threatened to kill one of the officers unless the other officer threw down his weapon and surrendered to the two criminals. To save the life of his brother officer the perception challenged officer complied. It didn't work out. The brother officer was murdered anyway. Some great teacher once said, 'Whoever will save his life shall lose it,' or words to that effect.

To my great surprise, both ladies rebuked me for not sympathizing with hostages who through no fault of their own find their lives threatened.

"How would you save them?" they demanded.

I answered speaking slowly and clearly,

"Saving hostages by agreeing to play negotiation games with criminals breeds ever growing numbers of hostages and criminals. Can't you see how it is increasing exponentially?"

Fell on deaf ears. I guess if you don't have testosterone you can not understand logic. I then decided not to continue with my well thought out plan to upgrade training of the cadets at the police academies by showing films of the East Side Kids also known as Bowery Boys.

When in trouble Leo Gorcey, Huntz Hall, Whitey or one of the gang would say something like, "Routine #6, fellas," and this urban youth gang would proceed to defeat their captors with some rehearsed strategies that could never be anticipated by the bad guys. They used prepared routines for feigning faints to foil the felons. Routine #6 might be vomiting or shouting 'Look over there!' or using some convenient prop or impediment to distract and disrupt. It put the bad guys on the defensive, unexpected motions going on and not knowing how to react.

When we returned to Susan's that evening I offered to take both of them out to supper. We went over to the Huntley Hotel on Second Street. It has an outside glass elevator to a roof top restaurant with a nice view of the Pacific, the beach, the pier, and downtown Santa Monica. We asked for a table near a window on the Second Street side but the hostess was saving all six of their presently empty tables for larger parties. A party of three doesn't rate a good table. I tipped the minimum later. I hope the 24 ghosts at those six tables tipped her much more than I did. They had the view seats.

Anyway we had a booth on a raised platform where we all three had our backs to the wall and could watch the other patrons and whatever glimpses of the sky there was. Every few moments we could see airliners from LAX about five or six miles away traversing the lower left window to the upper right corner of the window as they were taking off over the ocean.

SHE had thoughts I could almost read at seeing the airliners taking off toward the land of her birth. She didn't comment, but there was a look in her eyes that suggested nostalgia.

After dinner it was just a short drive, a couple blocks, to the Santa Monica Pier. I drove out onto the pier parking. It's more expensive but I was trying to show them a good time. I don't think ladies wearing heels appreciate walking forever and climbing staircases to save five dollars, as my father would have done in that situation. SHE and Susan studied the souvenirs in the curio shops. I had a chili dog and a magnificently red strawberry flavored shaved ice cone while we watched the breakers perpetual rolling onto the beach.

That's shaved ice, not a snow cone. The ice is very fine and melts so good on your tongue. In Little Tokyo Mitsi and I get them every summer when they set out the equipment and blocks of clear ice to shave. Mitsi and her friends sometimes get a ladle of red beans on their shaved ice.

MMM: Yummm.

As we stood out there on the pier watching the whitecaps roll to shore I thought again about the power of those waves that could generate electricity if anyone wanted them to. Whenever Mitsi and I stayed at the Miramar Inn the same thoughts would occur to me. Very powerful punches behind those surf rollers, due to the winds, tides, earth's rotation, or all of the three, I don't know.

The rest of the month I didn't see them much. SHE was being taught driving by Tom Nishinaka and after all, it was his Maxima. Susan said he had quit smoking and gambling and bought a lot of new clothes and spruced up his haircut and general appearance. He seemed intelligent enough if not well-read. He had dignity and good manners. It was obvious he was hoping to become closer acquainted with the young lady recently arrived from across the Pacific.

I see from my calendar that we four met again on June 25th. It was a dinner SHE prepared for Susan, Tom and me in Tom's apartment. SHE seemed to know her way around his kitchen and she prepared several dishes while we three made idle conversation in the living room. SHE could have free rein because Susan is not the domestic type and didn't want to intrude in the kitchen.

Speaking just for myself, it was my best meal of the year. She succeeded in capturing classic flavors that I have missed since I left home at seventeen for the mess halls of boot camp. I won't try to describe it but her gourmet approach must have been care in selection of ingredients, care with the spices, and impeccable timing. I remember how I had to teach Mitsi that it is necessary to use salt and pepper on hamburger patties, not just fry the ground meat.

> MMM: Well, I try but some of us have it and some of us don't. I realize that food preparation is not my *forte* -- the -te is silent.

I was again astonished how SHE is just too, too good to be true. Tom said, "SHE has magic hands. She touches a dish and makes it amazingly flavorful and purely perfect."

I guess he had some experiences with her culinary skills before that night, lucky fellow.

Astonishing again was our use of tea as the dinner and after dinner beverage. It was the choice of all four of us. I only drank coffee once in my life. It was on guard duty at Camp Pendleton on a cold, foggy night and the Officer of the Day came around with a thermos of hot coffee and some styrofoam cups and said,

"I brought you some hot coffee, private."

I was too shy to say, "No, thanks for driving out here with it at 2 AM, but I never touch the stuff."

He watched as I swallowed it down the hatch and forced a smile. That stinky brew stayed for thirty-six hours in my gullet. I never learned to drink beer either. Sour, bitter stuff. My dad liked it but when I gave it a taste it made no sense to me at all. Mormons don't drink coffee or beer and they serve in the military. Did the Officer of the Day look at my file to see if I wasn't a Mormon, or was he oblivious to making a social *faux pas*?

Now that I think about it, commercials on radio and television always insisted we keep our mouths kissing sweet. In retrospect the persons I found with offensive breath were probably the coffee drinkers. That boiled bean juice has a nice aroma when it is freshly prepared but the smell later emanating from the mouth and throat, at least in my experience is yuck. Some people I knew drank coffee and smoked cigarettes at the same time.

I shudder to think that I could have dated such a person and leaned in for a kiss. I must lead a charmed life. Truthfully, though, I didn't date much. I was more of a Jughead than an Archie. Oblivious to the typical social life of the high school years. Hm. That fleeting thought conjured up a picture of Nick Cufflett as Reggie Mantle with his shiny slick haircut. It's probably blow dried in contemporary issues of that periodical.

When I was serving at Pendleton in the 50s with the great American decathlon champion Bob Mathias, some local Oceanside marines drinking in an Oceanside bar decided they ought to treat some freezing civilian in the heartland to their lifestyle, giving him a break from the bitter winter back east. They decided to pick someone at random and make him their local celebrity of the week.

The ranking officer suggested they choose some fellow from the Tri-I-State area and someone yelled out Peoria. He said 'now someone with a common name like Smith, Jones, or --- and another guy yelled out Miller. Fine and now a first name and another guy yelled out Melvin. In those days MAD Magazine used Melvin as a silly gag name. The goofy looking kid on the cover with the 'What, Me Worry Face' was Melvin. A comic satire on Tarzan was Melvin of the Apes.

'Izzat OK with everyone?' Yeah! So this captain of the bar fellowship got on the innkeeper's telephone, asked the information operator in Peoria for the number of good old Melvin Miller, old buddy, old pal. There happened to be a Melvin Miller in Peoria --what are the odds?

-- and he answered the phone. The officer in charge of the committee assured him this was a legitimate call, some marines wanted to fly him out to Oceanside to enjoy the beach with them for a fortnight. The guy agreed to come. It was a pretty generous offer.

They went to the local newspapers and got publicity and donations for this stunt including Mamie Van Doren to meet Miller's plane wearing a glamorous gown and fur stole. With media photographers taking pictures for the news she ran to greet his arrival and kissed him shouting Melvin! Melvin! He became an instant celebrity in Oceanside.

They got him a room at the inn they favored, a beach chair and a beach umbrella with his name stenciled on them. Melvin Miller, in the sun and sand, sipping some libation with a little umbrella in it for the newspapers and also for souvenir pictures to send home. I'm pretty sure at least the Oceanside Blade-Tribune featured the story and pictures prominently.

One of their fun ideas involved a gambling pool as to which alcoholic beverage Miller would choose first and which label it would be. There would be a dozen beer labels, and many more liquor labels. It made the event more meaningful for the group. Miller was a family man about fifty and had a supervisory job in a Peoria factory. I don't think he had served in any military outfit.

He was a good sport about being made fun of, if that was the intent: Melvin from Peoria. But he disappointed his hosts by informing them he was a teetotaler. There are a few of us back there you know. I never heard about how they settled up on the beverage pool. I don't think water or soft drinks were choices.

Susan had touted Constant Comment tea and SHE found it exotic and delicious. It's also one of my favorite teas. Black tea with orange and spice you know. I've found out that Constant Comment was the inspiration for the line: *She gives you tea and oranges that came all the way from China* in Leonard Cohen's Suzanne.

Cohen is my idol. He's amazingly inventive in music and lyrics. For example he doesn't say 'everyone wants love.' Instead he says 'everyone wants a box of choc-lats and a long stem rose -- everybody knows.' He doesn't say 'western civilization' he says 'from that cross on top of Calvary to the beach at Malibu.' That takes in 2,000 years of history and pretty much of the geography, eh? Oh, yes, he is Canadian Jewish.

While sipping tea I thought about a time, at least twenty years ago, back in the 50s. Jack Kerouac wrote about different teas in his novel The Dharma Bums. We tea drinkers need such icons to validate our beverages. Coffee people have Joe DiMaggio, Danny Thomas and Mrs. Olson. Beer people icons are ubiquitous especially among professional football players who evidently need those calories to beef up. You don't see basketball players touting beer. Their game depends on reflexes and finesse.

The two weeks passed into three and SHE made no effort to return to her husband who presumably had returned to their apartment. Nothing was said among the four of us about the situation. We just carried on as usual.

It was a pleasure to dine with these young people and hear their conversations. It seemed to me that those three were natural friends and I was an older brother or an uncle or something. I no longer had to worry about improper thoughts or temptations. I was safely out of the situation and yet still privy to the drama that was still present in all of our minds. How is this going to play out?

MMM: I know Susan only from a few holiday family gatherings. Although we are both educators we are in different disciplines. Hers is Science, mine is Language Arts. I've never met Tom Nishinaka. He is a Nisei and I am an Issei even though we may be the same age. Jay has no need of common interests to talk to anyone about anything. I'm more withdrawn or aloof and might possibly appear as snobbish. It's not true. You can ask anyone. Anyone that matters.

Chapter Four

July

For the Fourth of July celebration, I joined the three of them at the Santa Monica pier for fireworks over the water. It was wall to wall people so we strolled about a mile and a half to the beach rather than be saddled with trying to park a car. The aerial bombardment as was spectacular as usual. The crowds were beautiful, colorful, and respectful.

We three natives were proud to show our visitor the patriotic rites of pomp, music and excitement of our Bicentennial-plus-three-years independence anniversary.

The words in the Star Spangled Banner were written after F. Scott Key witnessed a bombardment over water from aboard a ship off Fort McHenry. It suddenly occurred to me that seaside celebrations like this one in Santa Monica contain some elements, some atmosphere, of that original firefight for Independence.

Back in the mid-west it's the practice wherever possible to hold the fireworks shows over a pond or lake. One of the benefits is the colorful reflections in the water and another benefit is fire prevention by spent rockets as they fall into the water. All along the beaches in California the fireworks shows pack the crowds. I've enjoyed them at Long Beach as well as Santa Monica's pier.

It gets cool in the evenings by the ocean. Oddly enough, when my father visited one summer from Illinois we took him to the Rose Bowl at least twenty miles inland to watch the shows and we almost froze to death on the Fourth of July, shivering in the night air in our light windbreakers!

Mitsi was in Northern California for a week's seminar at the Monterey Defense Language Institute. That school has changed its name several times. She taught there when it was the Army Language School at Monterey. She called me the following day in the late afternoon, and seemed to be missing me while enjoying the reunion with old colleagues and friends.

> MMM: Yes, we saw the fireworks at the Presidio, or fire flowers as they are called where I was born. Jay's birthday is July 7 and we celebrate the date with fire flowers in the night sky to mark the meeting of a boy star and a girl star that come together once a year in the sky every July 7. I reminded Jay that this would be the first time since we met that we would miss combining the star festival with his birthday and Independence Day.

After the fireworks we made our way back to Sakura Gardens. My car was there in the parking spot reserved for Susan. I would have said goodnight and started for home but Susan asked me to come in for a few moments to talk about something.

It turned out that July 10th was Tom's birthday. She wanted to surprise him with a Haagen-Dazs combination ice cream cake, and have me join SHE and herself in singing happy birthday. I said, "So what's the big deal, why do we need to discuss it?"

"I have an idea that needs your strong voice to pull off," Susan replied. "I have an alternative happy birthday song, and it requires three singers."

Susan explained that she wanted to use *Frere Jacques*, the French folk tune that everyone knows as *Are You Sleeping, Are You Sleeping, Brother John? Brother John? Morning bells are ringing, Morning bells are ringing, Brother John, Brother John.*

Susan had printed her suggested alternate words. SHE knew the tune and could sing it in the round if she was the leadoff singer and could be finished before the third voice came in. Susan wanted to be second, and nominated me as the third voice. She felt I could hold my own against the two female voices that were further along with their verses.

Our discussion was to practice singing the round and perhaps find a better word in the second line, since she was unhappy with the adjective for Tom:

> *It's your birthday, happy birthday*
> *Super Tom, Super Tom*
> *You deserve a break now,*
> *Here's ice cream and cake now*
> *Super Tom, Super Tom.*

Thinking it might work, we tested it as Susan wished. SHE first, then Susan, then me. SHE sang it shyly, softly. Susan started her 'It's your birthday' at the same time SHE reached 'Super Tom.' Then I came in with 'It's your birthday' when Susan started Super Tom.

Super was not the smoothest word but Landlord Tom was worse. At least 'super' had the connotation of the person you call for help when there's a problem in your apartment, eh? We tried to come up with something better. It should be two syllables. Dearest Tom seemed a bit too intimate for the scots-irish in Susan and me. I promised to think about it. We had six days to work on it. Now I could get in my car, return to my lonely digs, and perform some serious snoring.

I know a couple of traditional rounds: Down at the Station, Early in the Morning -- See the little Puffa-Bellies All in a Row, and Row, Row, Row Your Boat -- Gently Down the Stream. But my favorite is the Fugue for Tinhorns in Guys and Dolls. *I got the horse right here, his name is Paul Revere, and here's a guy that says if the weather's clear, can do--can do---.* Since Tom was a gambler I worked on it as an alternate song to what Susan had prepared, but was unable to finish it. I gave up when it dawned on me that they might not be as familiar as I am with the tune.

Six days later I did not have a better lyric for Susan, but I went over to Sakura Gardens to sing what Susan had written. Susan and I started to discuss about what to call Tom in the Frere Jacques tune. SHE came up with a novel idea.

"Why do we all have to use the same adjective for Tom? I could sing Dearest Tom, Susan could sing Landlord Tom, and you could sing, Frere or Brother Tom. Since our voices are overlapping the adjective probably wouldn't even be noticed.

It wasn't perfect but it just might work. We rehearsed it a couple of times and then Susan called and asked Tom to come up to her apartment. I wasn't paying attention to the call but I think she used a ruse such as 'I've got a leaking faucet or a backed up sink,' some such *faux* emergency. Tom came immediately and we presented the ice cream cake and candle and I joined the ladies in serenading the birthday boy. My solo voice came at the end of the fugue when I sang, *Frere Tom, Brother Tom.*

The ice cream cake was Burgundy Cherry and had some customized frosting that suggested Sakura Gardens Apartments. Tom made a wish and blew out the single candle that Susan lit while we were singing. Tom was beaming with pride at the unexpected recognition.

Tom didn't have the usual manager's apartment. He had built a two story home with a koi pond and aviary near the center of the triangular shaped complex. The pond and aviary were open to the tenants but could only be accessed through a double doorway that kept the birds from escaping or outside birds from entering. Actually there were only three or four birds in his aviary. He wanted some life in there but preferred the kind that stayed on their perch, and did not bother the plant life.

It might have been planned when he was married and expecting children some day. He could enter the area directly through his office door which was a part of his house as well. He landscaped the complex with the usual tropical plants as other apartments similar in size and location, but in far larger numbers plus additional colorful flowering plants making Sakura Gardens lush with vegetation.

It wasn't just thirty units around a pond, it was three buildings around a two story dwelling/office/maintenance shed, divided by actual gardens. His living quarters were on the second floor. If you've ever seen the bungalows area at the Beverly Hills Hotel you'll recognize the kind of privacy and ambiance he created. You are barely aware of your neighbors behind the screens of bushes and trees.

In the center of the three buildings he created a pump driven waterfall for the koi pond, and a series of runs for the koi that might remind them of the irrigation ditches where their ancestors were spawned.

The flat rocks for his waterfall were awesome in suggesting a natural mountain spring leading to the spill ledge for the water. There were benches, wrought iron chairs and chaises for resting in the shade by the pond in addition to another set of chairs resting in the sun by the swimming pool which was away on the other side of the pond/aviary area. Residents had a choice of shade or sun for their outdoor relaxing, reading, chatting or whatever.

I suppose the outdoor seats were for the benefit of smokers who wished to indulge their filthy habit without provoking their co-tenants. I never got around to broaching the subject with Tom, who had been a smoker, but there were some ashtray stands available near of the chairs. I hoped that there was a rule about no smoking inside the apartments. So many smokers set themselves on fire when they fall asleep with a lit tobacco stick, often causing death and injury to others when the building catches fire.

The swimming pool was on the other side of his residence and was not completely indoors but well protected from the wind. I appreciate that myself. The warm sun can be nice when getting out of the swimming pool. If we got out of the water into a shady area the wind could be too chilling, not to mention the wind carries dirt, leaves, and debris.

I recognized that these apartments were not erected simply as an investor's income producing project, but as an actual livable retreat from the commercialism all around them. I had to give the man credit for building and maintaining something more elegant than was necessary to create income. He had made a conscious effort to make his property nicer than it had to be for the neighborhood.

These thoughts occupied my mind as I approached my own digs on Bedford Drive. To some extent both apartment complexes were dictated by the city planning departments. But still, given a choice at the same rents, I would choose Sakura as more comfortable than good old 401.

Mitsi likes to look out at the street when in the kitchen and there is an oblique view of the street from the kitchen sink. However the good view was from the living room. Sakura was a retreat from the street. All windows in the three apartment buildings would have a garden view, mostly landscaping, maybe a bird or a neighbor taking a rest. I guess you could pay your money and you take your choice.

The next afternoon my phone rang. It was Nick Cufflett. He had my business card.

"Hey, old dad, let's have supper if you haven't started it yet. I'm buying at Benihana's."

"Sounds like an offer I can not refuse." I'm not really into Italian gangster stories but cannot resist using a Marlon Brando line whenever the occasion allows me to. "You wuz my brudder, Charlie, you should have taken care of me---"

Just to make some idle conversation Nick said, "By the way, have you heard the latest about Carter (meaning the president)?"

"Uh, no."

"Some of his enemies think they have him caught in a conflict of interest scandal. It's really big. He's named his daughter Amy to be Secretary of Peanut Butter!"

"Heh, heh," I forced politely. I was glad it was not about Rosalynn. She's aces with me. Bill Murray had that right on Saturday Night Live. Murray and I both lust in our hearts for this magnificent lady.

I told him I'd be there at Benihana's in an hour and he was agreeable with that.

I decided to dress up for this meal. I wore a button down shirt with a sports jacket and no necktie. I never, have never, owned or wore jeans. They've never worked their spell on me as they have in the rest of the world. Heavy twill work pants, yes, but never Levi's with rivets or their derivatives. It has something to do with comfort or flexibility. I'm amused at guys with tight jeans. What's the attraction? On workmen or cowboys it looks natural. On white collar people it looks affected, following the fashion herd.

I've also never wore a shirt with writing on it except once. I try not to be a fanatic and when my sister gave me a T-shirt promoting our hometown Fall Festival I added it to my undershirt wardrobe.

Benihana's is on Restaurant Row on La Cienega, across the street from Lawry's. Benihana requires six people at each chef's station to qualify for their dazzling show with dexterous displays of daring knife work. We waited at the bar for four more patrons to show up and qualify us.

I offered to cover the bar expenses and Nick didn't argue. We both ordered the house scotch and I ordered a Seven-Up chaser instead of water or seltzer. Nick raised an eyebrow but I was not intimidated. There is no scientific instrument on this earth that can measure how little I care about other people's attitudes about anything I drink or eat especially when I am paying for it. That's just me. When the Seven-Up came I poured the shot into the glass with the ice and stirred it. Ahhh. Now that's a good libation.

I once brought a bottle of Black & White Scotch (James Buchanan, By appointment to Her Majesty the Queen) to a BYOB party hosted by a young fellow in his early 20s. I was stunned when he poured some into a glass holding his grape Kool-Aid, so I know how people can become aghast at witnessing sacrilegious behavior like that. Still, Seven-Up is not Kool-Aid. You may quote me.

Nick then pulled out two Upmann cigars from his inside jacket pocket. "Since you're getting the drinks I'll provide the smokes," he said.

Cufflett told me the secret service provided JFK with H. Upmann Havana cigars purchased at overseas tobacconists and brought into this country in diplomatic pouches. Then he said he'd been in Toronto a week ago and picked up some Havana contraband to smoke locally, and subsequently found two sticks left in his suit jacket today, a perfect cover story. I might have done the same, given the circumstances.

"Let's burn the evidence," we mutually agreed.

I've found them myself up in Toronto. I didn't have to look far for them. But $10 is my limit for a cigar. They wanted $15 American money for each Havana stogie up there in Canada, even the ones that were not Monte Cristo, Cohiba or Partagas. Not my $15. I can do without them at that price. $15 is $15 and you may quote me again.

Even if I didn't enjoy the fragrance I would want to light up to honor the memory and genius of Rudyard Kipling. Once upon a time his betrothed had issued an ultimatum that he memorialized in his poem The Betrothed. Either those cigars go or forget about possessing her lovely body. He'd only known her a few months, but had served as a Priest of Partagas for many years. A woman is only a woman, but a good cigar is a smoke.

It turned out that Cufflett (poor puppy) was fishing for information from me. He said, "Didn't you tell me at our last meeting that you'd been to a garden party for Jane Fonda?"

I said, "Yes."

He said, "Was the food and entertainment good?"

I replied, "Perfectly acceptable. They hired first class caterers."

"How about entertainment; was there a dance band or ---?"

I said, "I think there was a music combo of some kind, no dancing."

"So it was guitar, bass, keyboards--drums---"

"Yeah," I answered.

Hoping to divert Nick's topic away from that fateful garden party, I said, "By the way, I hope this offer of dinner isn't an overture of any kind other than casual acquaintance. I mean you're a terrific looking guy, and if I ever want to switch from girls, you'd be the first, but I ---"

Nick forced a polite chuckle at my little whimsical feint. He answered, "Since you mention it, I'd like to think I could do better than an old married man type like yourself. But be on your guard, I haven't forgotten that French speaking Asian mama you showed me a picture of. What could be more erotic and exotic than hearing French phrases in passionate embrace with ---"

That's where I cut him off.

"OK, fine, *touché* already!"

But I am never one to leave well enough alone, so after remembering Mitsi's very natural and inbred affection for sushi I continued with, "I'm strictly a meat and potatoes guy and wouldn't think of eating fish bait, but if you've ever kissed a honey when she has just eaten some wasabi laced rice; that is a true kiss of fire. It has to be what Johnny Cash had in mind, only maybe he got his from Tabasco sauce and Cajun or Mexican ladies."

Nick replied that he was well versed in oriental cuisine. He said, "I haven't tried mixing wasabi with French kissing, but I once had a hot kiss I can still taste from a honey as she was eating raw ray. You see, they put some kind of spicy sauce on it which tends to cook the ray in a different sense of the word cook."

I could go on like this but you get the idea. He always one ups me. Have I mentioned it was starting to get on my nerves? He then proceeded to straighten me out about Johnny Cash and the Kiss of Fire. Johnny was being adulterous, leaving his wife for June, and they were both seriously fearful of suffering the literal excruciating eternal fires of hell but couldn't help themselves. That song was not intended as a metaphor.

We finally had a quorum for the chef's theatrics with our shrimp and filet mignon dinners. The other four patrons were boy-girl couples. I tried to ask the chef where he got his colorful hat, kerchief and apron sets because I know some barbecue guys who would appreciate that kind of unique outfit as a gift, but he just put me off as if I wasn't speaking English.

After dinner we went back to the bar for another round. Nick suggested we down two drinks, finish the cigars, and then proceed to his club for a massage before calling it a night. Naturally I drug my feet a bit. Sure, Mitsi has walked on my back a few times, and worked the kinks out of my neck, so I'm not exactly a virgin in that regard.

Nick said, "Old dad, I really think you need a full hour full body experience with a full professional."

I pulled out my billfold and said, "I can afford an hour but I don't know how to tip."

Nick said, "A $20 tip is good for a strong, deep muscle massage, but should you want a happy ending, there's an understanding that a minimum tip of $100 is expected. Minimum."

I had $200 in my billfold so I decided to go along and learn something new about hedonism. How can I complain about sybarites if I don't study them just a little closer? My father used to say, "Some things in this world you can engage in once as a philosopher. But if you do them twice, you are a pervert!"

That seemed to allow me a peek see, eh?

The club he had in mind was on the border of Beverly Hills with West Hollywood and I'm not sure which jurisdiction it was. It was upscale, however, and the cashier took my $40 for the hour and introduced me to a muscular looking man in a gym sweat suit behind her curtain.

He produced a clipboard for me to read and sign. It said, "Do you have any allergies, any heart, blood-pressure, breathing or any other health problems?" I wrote no and signed my name. He asked to see my drivers license and checked the name I had signed.

The guy led me to a locker room. Nick held back saying he'd meet me in the waiting room later. Said he had to wait for his special masseuse.

The masseuse I was assigned was a surprisingly attractive Amazon. She reminded me of Conan's girl friend in his Barbarian film, the one who could handle a broadsword with ease. She was taller than me, buxom (we used to say) with long, straight blond hair and she had a very friendly personality. I imagined she came here to be an actress, maybe poised at this very moment to join the crowded ranks of starlet. A job in this location must be a good way for ambitious pretty girls to meet movie people, huh?

She shook my hand in introducing herself (I've forgotten her name) and suggested I take a shower. As I was showering she opened the curtain and scrubbed my back and other parts that might be difficult for me to reach. This surprised me since no one among the feminine ranks, except for family and nurses have ever seen me naked. I enjoyed lingering under the spray just a bit longer than I do at home, making sure I was clean even between my toes.

She looked Swedish in my imagination, so maybe it was a Swedish massage. Doesn't that require a sauna first, though?

She had me lay down in the prone position on a table in a room with canvas divider cubicles. She spent a half hour on my spine, legs, and ankles with her very strong fingers. After the deep muscle probing she went up and down my body with judo chops such as I have dreamed of receiving from Diana Rigg.

The next half hour I was supine and she worked on my scalp, neck, and forehead, pressing down with her fingers from the middle of the brow to the sides. She pulled on each finger; she pulled on each toe, stretching them and then let them snap back into their regular position. It seems the purpose of massage is to get rid of all muscular tension and to stimulate the blood circulation, to the benefit of every place that she touches.

I was probably too uptight to get the full benefit, but I felt it was well worth the $40. Neither she nor I brought up the words 'happy ending' and therefore there was nothing to tell Mitsi about. When she finished she helped me sit up on the table, helped me into my underpants and then the rest of my clothes, holding my shirt open for my arms and then helping me button it. I was sitting on the table as she knelt at my feet to get my shoes and socks on. My mommy stopped doing that when I was five years old. I enjoyed this treatment.

She shook hands, smiled and again told me her name, and said, come again, as I gave her a $40 tip. If Nick suggested $20 then I would give $40 just so I could feel superior to a millionaire in money matters. She gave me a few more judo chops on both shoulders by way of saying God speed, old timer.

In the waiting room I had to wait a half hour for Nick to come out and drive me back to the parking lot on La Cienega to pick up my car where we had dinner.

He said, "We should do this more often," and I may have nodded agreement with a smile but I had no intention of repeating the session.

It was great. It made me feel immortal. It reminded me of when I was young, in the armed forces, feeling invulnerable and transcendent with the planet. I can remember stepping outside of any building on a cool evening in those days, and looking up at the night sky thanking God and my parents for creating my body. It felt good.

That one session might have added weeks to my life, or improved my skin, muscle tone and circulation, but I can't afford $80 on my own pleasure very often. Not to mention the eight glasses of scotch I had paid for; three for me and five for Nick, but who's counting? There are too many other places for those dollars, including my family, my creditors, civic obligations such as church and charities. But it's something we all should do once.

> MMM: I never knew about this particular boys night out or any details about a Swedish massage. He didn't need to keep it a secret. We don't consider it a threat to our marriage if a husband has some drinks and gets a bath and massage. Relaxation is helpful for all bodies. I've gone to a spa many times myself and used some of their methodology to help Jay relax at home as well. It's not as if he needed to hide the night out from me. It's very normal male behavior. And why does he say the $80 was for pleasure? He should have said it is for his health.

As we drove back to Benihana's to pick up my car (the Volvo -- it's really mine and Mitsuko's, not my sister in law's) Nick softly broke out a few bars of Down By the Riverside: *I met my little bright-eyed doll, down by the Riverside, down by the Riverside, down by the Riverside.* It's an old favorite of mine so I joined in but skipping a verse or two. *I asked her for a little kiss DBTR, DBTR, DBTR, she said have patience little man, I'm sure you'll understand, I hardly know your name. I said, well honey some sweet day, if you let me have my way, your name and mine will be the same -- Oh, yes, I meet my little bright-eyed doll,* etc. etc.

Nick seemed pleased at our mutual repertoire of songs. I was almost tempted to ask, 'did you really meet that fiancée of yours down by the riverside?' Well, Los Angeles does have a river but it's pretty dry most of the time. I bit my tongue instead. No use provoking a situation. Instead I said, "I met my little bright eyed doll in an extension class in French." He didn't pick up on that comment as an invitation to disclose where SHE had met him, so I let it drop.

Instead I inquired, "Haven't I seen you perform folk music with some pop group? Lemon Tree Very Pretty? Malaguena Salerosa? My Green Tambourine? Yellow Bird?" Bud and Travis? The Brothers Four? I guess it was intended as flattery to his musical presence.

"Naw!" was his answer. Then silence. Sealed off from information about his professional life, and sealed off from information about his so called fiancée. I guess he didn't like personal questions.

When I exited his Benz to enter my car he said, "We'll do this again. I'll work on my favorite show tunes. Be prepared!" Show tunes? Are heteros allowed to love show tunes? I like to think so. I have quite a repertoire myself.

A few days later I called Susan to see if SHE had worn out her welcome. She said, "We're just fine, she'll stay on with me for the foreseeable future."

I asked Susan if she knew pretty much where SHE was at all times, had she made any trips to see her husband, or anyone else, (Nick Cufflett?) She said no. She hadn't seemed interested in contacting her husband. She said SHE was anxious to become independent, though, and earning some money. She was making phone calls, scanning the job advertisements.

I said, "How about travel agencies? Aren't her bilingual skills an asset?"

Susan replied, "The agencies all demand computer familiarity these days, and she doesn't have those yet. We can enroll her in adult school in September but the summer classes are all filled up. Tom wants to see you, why don't you give him a call?" She gave me his phone number and handed me her phone.

Tom was happy to hear my voice.

He said, "You have really brightened my days with this SHE situation. I'd like to take you, Susan, and SHE to Las Vegas as my guests. We'll test the air conditioning in my new Chrysler, SHE can put in some time at the wheel out there in the desert, and we'll take in some shows.

Then I'll write off the hotel and entertainment expenses on my taxes by entertaining prospective investors in my business."

I begged off. Especially as an honest accountant, I begged off. Mitsi was back from Monterey and needed to know about my whereabouts. Tom went on to describe his idea of a three day, two night holiday. The girls would have their own room and Tom and I would bunk together. He wasn't hearing my no.

I conjured up a scenario in my mind of what he planned. He wanted to propose marriage to SHE over there, and Susan and I would be witnesses. He didn't have to say it. The desperation in his voice as he tried to convince me said it all.

"Tom, I really appreciate the offer, but you'll have to make do with just Susan, or she'll have to find a date to take my place. You must count me out."

"Fine, but do this much for me. Susan says SHE is looking for a millionaire. The equity in my apartments is worth more than that now. I net $60,000 a year more than I need for maintenance. I could net more if I was filling out a joint return."

"Oh, you romantic guy you," I answered. "You've convinced me to put in a word for you."

"Yes, try and get a sense of my chances, would you?"

I promised and I did. Not directly at first, but through Susan.

I told her some of what Tom had said.

"Oh, he's recruited you now? He's been feeling me out to feel her out, if you know what I mean."

"She could do a lot worse," I replied.

"She could do a lot better," Susan countered. "She and I have been thinking of signing up with a matrimonial agency that finds consorts for shy millionaires. Maybe I could catch one of her rejects. Or maybe one will say to me after I pitch her qualities, 'Why not speak for your self, Susan?' Could it happen? "

"It could happen," I flattered my cousin.

I've seen those introduction services in the classifieds such as Los Angeles Magazine. SHE and Susan tumbled a few points inside my head over this crass idea of cashing in on appearances for wealth. What have I got on my hands here, two gold diggers? Yeah, sometimes I ask the obvious. Some kind of compulsion, I guess.

I've lived too long. Growing up I believed in marriage as a sacred union of like minded interests, compatible beliefs, harmonious spirits, admiration for the other one's character and talents, shared virtues, and shared pleasures plus some kind of mystical subconscious attraction. Best friends to the nth degree. Now, in the twentieth century it's come down to materialism and get all you can or existentialism and get as many experiences as you can.

There's even a book somewhere called Trading Up that teaches the ladies how to improve one's place on the social ladder by finding richer men and then divorcing -- marrying upward. It can get depressing thinking the whole world has gone materialistic with a mantra of 'I've got mine, where's yours?' And 'devil takes the hindmost.' Equally depressing is the soulless experiences of existentialism.

The Old Testament sages predicted mankind's downfall a second time. The writers of Genesis knew full well about man's weakness for materialism over spiritualism.

Another point about Genesis that resonates with me is that we have two world powers threatening to destroy the world with fire and some prophets wrote about this happening over 2,000 years ago. Those holy men knew that the flood didn't wash away something in our blood, bones or genes, which is self destructive. They understood that water was useless in quenching fires in our blood and the next instructive cleansing would need to be a hotter louder lesson to get man's attention.

I used to laugh at the idea of men creating gods out of stone or metal and them bowing to them, offering sacrifices, worshiping such statues. Couldn't they see it was just a rock, a hunk of marble or a bronze god they shaped from a sand mold?

But it you think about it, these days we manufacture automobiles and worship them, bathe them, and caress them, and anoint them with carnauba waxy oil. Oh, yes, we know they are metal, leather, rubber and plastics, but they empower us with status and give us cachet over others less fortunate. We wear corporate and sports logos like primitive people wore religious amulets to show their loyalty or tribal connections.

I once read a novel by a secular Israeli who suggested the Hebrews fleeing Egypt were ashamed of appearing to be poor to the Bedouins or other peoples in the area. The Golden Calf they made from what jewelry they brought with them was to impress the neighbors with their wealth. They fully understood there were no supernatural powers or favors to be derived from this object.

That secular author suggested the Pillar of Fire they followed was the camp fire of Moses and the leaders. If you had thousands of people out in a wilderness and were moving along, you would need a pillar of fire and smoke to show the direction the rest of the camp was moving in. Those ancient Bible stories resonate with me as indisputable unvarnished truth.

What interpretation will future archeologists give to our toys that survive the elements? Totems or gods? We worship more than automobiles. The gun nuts are even more devoted to their toys, kissing, cleaning, caressing, and admiring them, praising their power and abilities to assist them and strike down their opponents. They even give them human names. Pat Boone's ancestor Dan'l carried Old Betsy, didn't he? There are other obsessions to material goods as well, as we see advertisements in the media for collectors of certain types of personal goods.

Jane Fonda's husband, Tom Hayden, wrote a book about our society using a quotation from Sitting Bull for the title: The Love of Possessions is a Disease with Them. That's a pretty perceptive observation by a fellow the early settlers regarded as a savage. I got Hayden's autograph in my copy of the tome.

Gandhi died with just two possessions, I've heard. One was his loin cloth and the other was the apparatus that he had built himself for spinning cotton into thread. He wanted to be an exemplar and we need not be that extreme, but until our food and shelter is distributed more fairly, we shouldn't be storing up more and more goods that we can't take with us when we go, eh?

The richer men become the more their personal space has to appear like a temple of old, on a hilltop to be closer to Heaven, for all the lowly people to look up to. Their offices must be the highest in their building, preferably in a corner with windows offering 150 degree views. Their homes and bedrooms must be gigantic. One of our downtown hotels has suites that have larger than king size beds for those VIPs. In fact I think there are two sizes above king -- Emperor and Despot. I read that once but it may not be true.

Ah, well. I took Tom's cause to heart and made an effort to reach SHE with his petition. In my mind, Tom Nishinaka was a prime candidate because he had proven his lack of ambition. SHE would never have to worry about his trading her for another. He lacked the energy. Apartments near the ocean will always be in demand. The electorate just last year protected their owners from property tax increases with Proposition 13.

Tom's property was a safe investment with what I considered plenty of spending money.

I suppose the bloom was off the rose for both SHE and Tom. They both had prior marriage partners. Neither expected magic and intoxicating romance. Well, maybe Tom did. And it turned out when I brought the subject up, so did SHE. I should be minding my own business.

Back in college one of my history professors said that continental colonial money did not say 'In God We Trust.' No way. It said, 'Mind Your Own Business.' Most immigrants in America came from Europe to escape government/religious controls as well as their neighbors nosiness. Neighbors in the old countries wanted to know your religion, your blood lines, your family connections or whatever.

Governments then, maybe now, collected taxes to subsidize the churches according to if you were Catholic or Protestant. They had to know your religion and agnostic or atheist was not acceptable. You could be burned at the stake for such paganism. In Spain these rituals were called *autos-de-fe*. Cremation while still alive. Anne Boleyn meekly submitted to having her head severed rather than endure a British version of *autos-de-fe*, and thanked Henry VIII for his kindness.

America was the place to make fresh beginnings with no inherited baggage. In God We Trust came around in 1956 along with Under God in the Pledge to the Flag, which I always felt uncomfortable with. I completely agree that loyalty to God is more important than loyalty to my country. I can see where someone wanted that added if they were pledging loyalty. It's just that I don't believe in being required to pledge loyalty to God in front of other persons. Our forefounders came here to escape government and religious officials inquiries into their beliefs.

If one wishes to pledge allegiance to the USA they must acknowledge God's supremacy over this nation? I think God's supremacy over all the nations in the world goes without saying or else He wouldn't be God! Isn't that so?

Some nonconformists insist their religion is Druid or Wiccan. "Ewwww, I'm a witch!" I believe in recognizing nonconformists certain rights, but not the right to dictate to the majority population that their traditional holidays cannot be celebrated in public offices because they would then feel left out. Jews, Moslem, pacifists, Jehovah's Witnesses do not participate in our traditions and then feel left out? They've chosen to be left out and yet to live among us. They need to be tolerant as well. Political correctness can go too far.

The Apostles Creed even has one or two words in it that make me uncomfortable. I'm just that kind of person. I take all the words seriously in sworn oaths. I had to use the word 'catholic' in there for example, and I asked my Sunday school teacher, 'Aren't we Protestants'?

The answer was: the word catholic in our Apostles Creed has a lower case 'c', not the upper case Roman Catholic 'c' so we can say the word. Catholic is derived from the Greek word for universal.

But in my mind how is anyone hearing my oath supposed to sort out upper case or lower case? Both Roman Catholic and Protestants call their faith universal? How can that be?

> MMM: I've told my husband many times, "you think too much!! You should try Zen, make your mind blank and open. Don't try too hard to solve riddles that have no solution."

SHE had three driving instructors, me, Susan, and Tom. She logged a lot of hours at the wheel. I got to be the one who took her to the DMV for the drivers test. Guess what? She passed. Now she was as free as any other person to come and go by herself, dependent only on her own resources and not another person's goodwill. We stopped for lunch at an IHOP and I asked what she thought of Tom Nishinaka.

She said, "He's been wonderful. He's been even more helpful than you've been, although, I never would have met him if not for you, so I just said something stupid."

"No, no," I insisted. "He's the man. Has he mentioned taking you and Susan to Las Vegas for a little holiday in that burning hot desert sun?"

"No."

"Well, he mentioned it to me, asking me to go with you and Susan, to see a couple of shows and some nightlife."

"But hasn't he given up gambling?"

"Las Vegas is a gambling center but you don't have to throw your money away. You can watch people of all kinds. You can be amazed at excessive conspicuous consumption, electrical lights and uses of neon. There are some magnificent food buffets. There are some razzle dazzle entertainment venues over there. You can see magicians, acrobats, dancers, tigers, orangutans doing tricks, re-enactment of historical events like the sinking of the Titanic, the shooting down of the Red Baron---"

Pause for a moment, and then, "And you can see people getting into instant marriage, no waiting period. Just drive in, pay the fees, hear the words, and pick up a legal document attesting to your matrimony."

Her face clouded very suddenly.

"I wouldn't want to do that," she said. "My first marriage was a sudden whim. I want to be engaged for several months and be thoughtfully deliberate for my next time at the altar."

You understand I'm paraphrasing her words but using quotation marks.

"I'm grateful to Tom, but I can't imagine spending the rest of my life with him in Santa Monica."

I didn't give up that easily. "He would be rock steady, though. He has at least a million dollars in net worth, although I haven't actually audited his mortgage or income taxes. He says he nets $60,000 a year for discretionary uses such as travel or material acquisitions. If I had a daughter and she asked me, I'd say I'm fine with that choice."

"I understand Susan had a romance that lasted several years. She would probably agree with you. But I haven't had any romance at all. Putting the choices on the table I'd see Tom as my third choice, passionate romantic love as second choice, and first choice would be a several million dollars in a bank account to acquire a great house or estate.

I have this vision of a mansion. It's not a vision of lazy luxury nor is it a castle in a wealthy area or with a fantastic view. In my dreams this big house is shared with many old retired people, or many orphans, or rescued animals. It isn't a selfish dream as you might think. I would be actively working there in some kind of capacity to make a better life for all of us."

The last part made me feel a little better. So the mansion was not a pure ego trip that she felt she deserved. She wanted to be gregarious and have plenty of stimulating interactions. Not my cup of oolong but someone needs to do it, maybe.

It even seemed a worthy goal when I thought about all the undeserving rich people there are. One idea from religion that I never accepted was that prosperity was a reward from God for being a good person. That is laughable on its face. My people believe in the adage: no good deed goes unpunished. We perform them stubbornly, proudly in spite of this credo.

In Sunday school they told us that it is easier for a rich man to ride a camel through a needle than it is for a rich man to enter Heaven. Doesn't everyone know this? Didn't they go to Sunday school?

Anyway SHE was now free to come and go due to attaining the magical driver's license I.D. card. It would be arriving in a few weeks by mail so maybe in a few weeks I'd get a chance to see her birth date or if the picture on it did her justice. In a very a large percentage of licenses the pictures make us look like criminals; at least on all the ones I've collected through the years. When the ladies don't want you to see their cards it can be because of the age disclosure, but it can also be the unflattering likeness thereon.

In fairness to Tom I came back to the topic one more time to impress SHE about how security should be a factor in her search for a more suitable mate. Assets invested in stocks could collapse, but real estate is pretty much permanent. And Tom has demonstrated he's an extremely decent and generous man. She didn't answer; she looked away from me.

The diplomatic corps missed an opportunity when they failed to recruit me out of college. I am the very soul of discretion and have never changed anyone's position on any issue.

> MMM: 'The diplomatic corps!' I consider that a subtle dig at my father. Jay has often been critical of political diplomacy in current events. He lacks any knowledge of Tao, or positive inaction, letting nature take its course. It is difficult for many people to see that inaction can be honorable. A famous example: The 1930s Dust Bowl in the prairies west of the Mississippi was an unintentional result of farmers

breaking up thousands of years old sod. Nature's precedents should have been considered. Some politicians wanted to strengthen this nation by building up agriculture and spreading the population out into the new lands. Tao, and the new lands rebelled. The word that comes to mind is: counterproductive. Actions can be counterproductive.

Nick called again a week later. Said we had communed with the sybaritic side of life the other night with Benihana steaks, cigars, scotch, and massage. He said, "Have you been neglecting your physical health? You look tough enough, but from all our conversations I suspect you have a sedentary life style."

It was true enough. But I defensively replied, "The marines gave me a workout that's lasted many years. I never found any use for the one armed pushups that I learned so well. It is quite possible that I've lost my edge."

"Just as I thought," Nick said. "Do you belong to a health club?"

"Mitsuko does. She likes to run the indoor track and she likes to use the treadmill. Actually there probably aren't many ladies in the Westside that aren't into maintaining top physical form."

"She can't do it for you. You have to sweat a couple times a week at least."

I answered, "It's just boring. I believe along with Neil Armstrong that our hearts are programmed for just so many beats and it seems a shame to wear them out in boring movements."

"How did you come to join the marines?"

"Why do you need to know that?" It's my stock answer to queries that appear personal. Anyway I retorted, "I was taking judo lessons at the Moline YMCA when I was a senior in high school. The instructor just happened to a recruiting sergeant, OK?"

"Yes, I thought you were sort of phlegmatic."

"I hope that's not an insult. I thought we were friends since last week's evening on the town."

"Oh, the word just means even tempered, laid back, almost passive."

Dang! The guy has a better vocabulary than I do. Who would know the word phlegmatic?

"Tell you what," he continued, "I also find exercise boring if there's no one doing them with me. Why don't you join me at my dojo and we'll warm up and maybe exchange some throws."

I couldn't come up with an excuse so I agreed. He gave the address and the time. I rummaged around for my *gi* and was surprised at how tight it fit. Guess I had put on some pounds since marriage and a life style with regular meals.

When I showed up Nick was on the mats doing some crawling exercise -- where you pretend you don't have any use of your lower body. You must pull yourself forward by extending the arms flat out and exerting the muscles therein to drag all your weight. Can't use your elbows. I was not surprised to see that he wore a brown belt. I had the white belt that came with my *gi* when I bought it for use at the Y. I may also disclose that his *gi* fit him like it had been designed for his body. It was well worn. He jumped up when he saw me, bowed to the sensei and left the mats to talk.

The dojo didn't have any showers; it was just a store front. There was a small room with a sink and toilet and a bench for changing clothes, though. I changed and approached the mat, bowed to the sensei. There were four other guys doing rolls and slapping the mat. That's the standard exercise for warming up. I did ten rolls and slaps. Nick sat on the sidelines cooling off. Not a hair was out of place. Probably lacquered. When I completed some other warm up routines that I remembered I bowed off the mats and joined Nick on the bench. He said, "When you get your breath let's do some throws."

"Your brown belt is telling me you've had many many more falls than me," I replied.

"You still working on your first one thousand falls?" he asked rhetorically.

He'd be the sensei and I could rack up some falls. He demonstrated his shoulder throw. It's the most popular throw in tournaments. It was surprising how he lifted me up and over his shoulder. I'm sure I outweighed him. He let me throw him a few times. Then to redeem myself I said, "Fine. Now show me your *tomoe-nage.*"

"Holy moley, Jay! Aren't you rushing our relationship?"

"You know exactly what I said," not being able to match him in repartee.

Most beginners are apprehensive of *tomoe-nage.* It's also called the cowboy throw because in many B western brawls one cowboy falls on his back taking advantage of the other guy's lack of balance as he comes rushing forward. He gets one boot into the guy's stomach and both hands on the guy's jacket lapels and thrusts him via that one leg and two arms overhead in a somersault. I've never seen it done in a tournament. I suspect it's easy to do in practice with a cooperative partner but more difficult to time correctly with a resistant competitor.

As a beginner back at the Y it looked scary to me, but after the first throw I relaxed and enjoyed the flight. If I have a passive personality that proves it. I could be a practice dummy. The feeling was like having my dad throw me in the air and catch me when I was little. It's an easy flight with no exertion on my part.

Nick sent me flying a half dozen times and my weight started to get to him. We both sat down on the sideline bench again. I was beginning to doubt my first misgivings about this gentleman. Maybe it was the fact that he smelled of honest sweat and not cologne.

"Thanks for coming," he said. I was surprised that he hadn't pumped me again for information about SHE. He must have considered me a blind alley. Was he actually concerned about my well being -- or to entice me into his life style? Massages, exercises, scotch and cigars? Maybe he had something in mind but decided to put it off for another time.

We agreed to go our separate ways to respective homes for proper showering and relaxation. I had parked my Volvo near his Benz so we walked along together silently. He threw me a little wave goodbye and I threw a snappy salute back to him, thinking I'd misjudged him all along.

I've mentioned running into celebrities in these parts. I want them to know I recognize them, but I don't want to bother them with hello, I know who you are, good to see you chit-chat. In its stead I now salute them as if they are officers in our Armed Forces. It acknowledges that I know them and respect them or their body of work. I only salute if they are looking at me to see if I recognize them or might say something. I don't hold the salute for a return. Just a quick gesture.

Chapter Five

August

I just caught a flash from the past, Teahouse of the August Moon. Where did that come from?

"All moons good, August moon little older, little wiser," someone says in the stage play or the film. That's something we don't see often enough on the late show movies, Marlon Brando in ethnic makeup as Sakini, that wily Okinawa native saying,

"Life makes pain, but that's good because pain makes man think, thinking makes man wise, and wisdom makes life endurable."

Pain? Oh, wait. I get it. Zen. Don't think about it.

We four had one more meeting before their scheduled get-away over in the Silver State's desert. Tom invited me to join them for a dinner at Yamashiro in Hollywood, on a hill above the Magic Castle, a private club for master magicians. Movie producers of the Marlon Brando and Red Buttons film, Sayonara, used it for a scene, pretending it was in Japan. It has a koi pond, some outdoor seating, and a magnificent view of the Hollywood area below which naturally did not appear on camera.

After my first visit I wondered why Brando never purchased it outright to convert it to his personal showplace of home. That is something that I might do if I was in his place with a job mostly in Hollywood film factories. The answer is probably because it is too accessible. Hollywood tour buses or too many fans would not allow him any true enjoyment of the location. An island in Tahiti could be more restful.

Tom announced that he was taking the girls to Las Vegas for a couple of days for Susan's birthday, no surprise except for the date and hotel reservation. He was sparing no expense, it was Caesar's Palace. I wished them well and gave them each one quarter from my pocket to invest in some promising looking payouts, should they discover a slot machine during their sojourn in the desert. I'm not a gambler but prefer not to be a fanatic about anything as I tend to say often.

The main topic of conversation at Yamashiro was music. Susan's roots are also scots-irish from the mid-west. OK, let me say it another way. We are two hillbillies living on the west coast now. When we think of the violin we think of the fiddle our mutual grandparent played.

One favorite little Okeh recording on 78 rpm shellac that we both remembered was Red Ingle's 'Pagan Ninny's Keeper Goin' Stomp.' On the label it credits a caprice variation known as Perpetual Motion by Nicolo Paganini. Through the years it has galled me to see that title miswritten from Keep'er Goin' Stomp to Keeper Goin' Stomp, which completely fouls up the connection to perpetual motion and suggests a dancing insane asylum warden. Somebody didn't know their apostrophes. Keep 'her' as in keep the music going. Her is a pronoun rendered as 'er!

The term perpetual motion got Tom to raise a scientific question to Susan, the science teacher, about the power of the surf and tides to generate electricity. He said, "My folks told me if I should ever discover perpetual motion I could hook up electric generators and get free energy."

Scientific Susan was quick to answer that she and I had often thought about that every time we went to the beach. You can hear the power, it just needs a transformer.

It is probably natural for people living on the coast to think about. That continuous wave power should be jacked up to dynamos to generate electricity. The only reason they had not been exploited was, the right people could not think of a way to become even more rich and powerful from that cheap inexhaustible power source. The technology would be easy, the making it profitable for a few 'investors' would be the tricky part.

Sometimes I regret not studying law -- the law of discovery. When Europeans explored this continent for gold and eventually found petroleum they won possession of an ocean of energy by right of discovery. That might float but I seem to remember our government giving tax breaks to the billionaire discovery-owners because they were depleting 'their' resource.

Oil Depletion Allowances they called it. Using up a nonrenewable resource creates a tax deduction. Profits from discovery and exploitation of petroleum and then reimbursed for their future profits because the supply was limited! I tend to believe the senators from Oklahoma and Texas might have been instrumental in sandbagging that particular wealth for the few.

So even though we see, feel and sense the power in the surf and tides and know they can generate electricity we have not established ownership of that true perpetual motion. Not to mention the winds that flow onshore and offshore every day without fail, and no one to harness their power. The world is waiting, waiting for the right people to patent and exploit it. Couldn't ever be a public utility, could it? No, we can't let all citizens benefit from clean God driven energy. Has to be a concession grant to an entrepreneur developer!

Maybe I should be the one to file a claim with the government that I have discovered energy, just like the oil prospectors did. My energy would not pollute the world and I would pay full taxes on the sale of electricity, since the source would never be depleted, eh? My source is not underground, it is in the air and surf. That must be the catch.

Actually, I worked at a sand and gravel company once and one of the workers on the mill that grades and sorts the aggregates saw gold glinting in the air as the mill operated, filed a claim, set up a gunny sack rig to pick off the gold dust, and derived a little profitable side income on his boss' property. The owner of the property with sand and gravel hadn't claimed the gold. Who would have thought?

But getting back to Red Ingle, Pagan Ninny's Perpetual Motion caprice jogged my memory about his many hillbilly ditties that often included sophisticated songstress Jo Stafford. One of her big hits with Ingle was Tim Tay Shun, which made her a dad burn slave. Temptation! The word fitted Tom and myself. Temptation! The flip side of that shellac was Cigareets and Whiskey and Wild, Wild, Women. They don't write songs like that anymore. Maybe they should. Ingle called it a preachment about the wages of sin.

SHE confessed a passion for Paganini's First Violin Concerto. It was a popular staple for violin virtuosos when she was a teenager. Tom had no ear for music and watched wide-eyed as the three of us threw the name around mentioning various recordings. My first vinyl disc of it was Zino Francescatti's version. I have at least six more recordings. But it seems the first version one hears is the one you stick with as the definitive. Same with alcohol. The label you start with is the one you come back to, or so it seems to me.

I even tried writing a bio-pic for the movies using the second movement as soundtrack as the opening credits unfold to Pagan Ninny on a podium looking demonic and rock star-ish from his opening notes after the orchestral introduction. Wow, what drama! I visualized Henry Silva in the role. What intensity that actor has!

While driving home alone as Tom drove Susan and SHE back to Sakura Gardens I came up with Al Pacino as another possibility for Paganini. Still, Silva would be my first choice.

We may have talked the topic to death but this discussion spilled over into my conversation in my next meeting with Nick Cufflett. A few days later Nick and I got together and he was still fishing for information from me, this time on a fishing expedition with actual pescatory ambitions.

We met at Jerry's Famous Deli in the Marina Del Rey for breakfast. Nick said another man would be joining us but he was alone at a table when I came in at the appointed hour.

I asked him if he'd heard about Andrew Lloyd Webber's recent adaptation of those caprices for Julian, his younger brother, called Variations on a Theme of Paganini for Cello and Rock Group. I had the recording. I lamented that it wasn't getting proper air play and blamed it on being a novelty that does not fit any radio stations format -- neither classical nor rock.

Nick said, "That argument doesn't hold water. It is both classical and rock and therefore should be getting twice the airplay!"

He went on to say that American classical musicians generally despise Lloyd Webber for being popular. He said in Europe that particular recording is well regarded and appreciated. In Europe classical music is applauded for being popular and accessible to the listeners. Americans seem to be tired of the old sounds by dead white Europeans and want to rewrite musical motifs with experimental sounds. There's a lot of ego involved.

I mentioned Philip Glass and his brittle sounding The Photographer. It is a study in minimalism but Mitsi and I endured hearing it several times. During the first hearings I almost wanted to claw my face off, but it caught on with us and now we tout it as an excellent, modern, potential classic standard that everyone should have a chance to appreciate. This time Nick had no knowledge of that particular piece, only knowledge of Glass' name and prominence.

> MMM: Jay and I are converts to Philip Glass' new music. Not all new music is good, not all classical music is good. This piece recorded by the Philip Glass Ensemble is really good.

I gave myself one point for that. Getting back to Lloyd Webber we both agreed that if we were obligated to exchange our souls for someone else living at the same time, we would not mind being Andrew Lloyd Webber instead of our present selves. We could endure it. He's earned a few shekels doing really useful projects.

Nick then challenged me, "Andrew Lloyd Webber or Hugh M. Hefner?"

I went with Webber, Nick went with Hefner. I don't know Hef's ancestry, I've heard he was a Methodist, but I know Webber's Northern British roots. We have to be distant cousins, and I'm proud of him. I tend to think of Hefner as having a tiger by the tail and unable to let go. In the first few issues he demonstrated a good intellect. After that he was forced to commune daily with non-intellectual bunnies. That brought in the money. He was forced to live with it.

The original concept for Playboy was to salute common male fantasies on the slut next door. Somehow success twisted the thrust of the publication to exhibitionist ladies. Letters to the editor shouted, "Show me! Show me! Or show my daughter! Show my wife! Show my girl friend! Take a gander at these assets!" As if it was a high honor to be chosen as a playmate, a temporary sex toy for a month.

If any letters suggested 'Show my mother' I missed them but I'm almost certain they must exist. Still, we read history about morality in primitive times and think we've made progress. I think it's the lazy gene. We want to receive money or fame for nothing more than showing what we were born with.

They expect contacts with wealthy playboys, modeling agencies or movie moguls based on superficial temporary flesh appeal. What a twisted dream! While Webber has been generously productive, enriching our lives with beautiful sounds and inspirational emotions, Hef praises and touts superficial, empty materialism to sell corporate products.

> MMM: I'm too tired to edit that nonsense again. Just skip over it, all right?

Nick told me that one particular recording last year by the German duo Baccarat called Yes sir, I Can Boogie was the number one popular song in Europe and yet it is almost unknown in this country. He said air play is in control of very few hands and if those hands do not have the royalty rights, we won't hear it played. That explained a lot about popular music to me. I'm sure he's right. Dare I say this: Didn't the mafia control juke boxes at one time? Was that from history class?

"I want you to meet Bryan Jennings," Nick said. "He'll be joining us on the boat. Have you done any salt water fishing?"

"No. It is on the list of ambitions to accomplish that I wrote up at age twelve, but it's still untried. I haven't even dropped a line over the pier as you see so many of our neighbors doing."

There are always people fishing off the pier at Santa Monica, Malibu, Torrance, or anywhere along the coast. My problem is what would I do with a fish if I caught it? I once had an opportunity over at Catalina Island to snag a flying fish. I don't know if they migrated here from Mandalay or were they all over the globe. The Catalina coast is thick with them, but the locals say they are not decent eating. Mitsi eats fish but has no interest in cleaning and ingesting fish from Santa Monica Bay. We've both seen the sewers emptying into the ocean near there.

Another time I tried to catch the elusive grunion that lay their eggs at high tide in the sand locally under a special full moon. Fish and Game protects them from being netted. You may only use your hands to catch and put them in buckets. They were always out of my reach just down the beach. That's been a common theme in my life, something always just out of reach. Close but no cigar. Just out of reach. Mitsi, that could be my epitaph if the occasion arises. Here lies Jay G. Miller, just out of reach.

> MMM: Oh, I'm sure we could do better than that! Let's make it a haiku!

"Bryan Jennings is an enthusiastic salt water sailor but he's meeting with us to discuss politics. He and I have been on a few ad hoc committees together and we are looking to recruit more familiar faces to smooth out the mechanics of organizing action groups. Someone we can trust who won't be a police provocateur or informer," Nick said.

It's a shame that the police are often the tool of entrenched conservatives of the worst kind. Wherever social progress has happened it has been at the expense of broken heads and shoulders from the law's truncheons. I was a witness to a police riot in Chicago in 1968. One of Chicago's prosperous citizens, Hugh Hefner, was an innocent bystander there who felt the wrath of pro-war/anti-hippie police officers on his physical head and shoulders.

Think of Gandhi and his nonviolent sit-ins to improve social conditions in his country. Think of Dr. Martin Luther King Jr. chased with fire hoses and dogs for daring to suggest all citizens ought to have equal protection or equal opportunity or equal access under the laws of this country.

As we ate breakfast Mr. Jennings arrived, ordered coffee and Danish, and we three soon set out in Mr. Cufflett's Mercedes for his yacht.

When we got to the moorings I looked quickly at the name to see if it was named for SHE. It wasn't. Ha! But it turned out that it wasn't Nick's yacht. It was Jennings' boat.

Nick had deferred to Jennings because he had the better fishing gear and accoutrements already on board. Nick said, "This way we won't stink up my little boat which I use more for pleasurable relaxing, romantic trysts and such. Fishing can be exhausting if you work at it."

Jennings had an auxiliary motor so we putt putted out past the breakwater and then the two of them set the sails. They knew of a spot where we could stop and drop our lines into some kind of underwater reef where the fish like to hang out.

To my mind the whole purpose of fishing has always been for relaxing, catching some rays with a pole, bobber, and hook as a cover for taking a nap. Catching a fish would be a distraction. But with these salt water types, fishing was aggressive and participatory. More like hunting.

But then, isn't hunting also a relaxing way for men to get together in some fresh air away from female detractors to drink beer and tell tall tales using salty language? I'm not qualified to say since I'm not an active participant.

I asked, "So, Mr. Jennings, are you a judoka?"

"Of course," he replied. "It's the manliest sport in its field. Karate is just ballet dancing. No one dares contact an opponent with those wild kicks. I tried it and went back to Judo. After I got my black belt I learned the chokeholds pretty well."

"Uh-oh," I was over my head. Chokeholds for submission are reserved for black belts only. Shouldn't have brought it up, but was just curious if he and Nick were dojo mates. Even so, I had obligated to reply something to his stated preference for judo. I said, "Yeah, karate and tai-kwon-do are beautiful to watch but I don't know how much good they'd be in street fighting. Where I grew up kicking was only for women and Frenchmen."

MMM: It's called *savate* (the -e is silent.)

Jennings sought to focus the small talk on his agenda. He inquired if I had ever suffered mistreatment by the police. I was ashamed to say that my only unpleasant encounter had been when they physically carried me from a sit-in scene when I went limp. Jennings suggested that put me between himself and Cufflett who had never been assaulted. He asked me feel the bumps on his head where nightsticks had temporarily persuaded him not to pursue freedom of speech in America.

It may have been due to the sea air or possibly the discussion back at Jerry's Deli, but I started singing some Pirates of Penzance inside my head. To whit: *When a felon's not engaged in his employment (his employment) or pursuing his felonious little plan (little plan) 'is capacity for innocent enjoyment ('cent enjoyment) is just as great as any honest man.*

That was in my head. *Sotto voce* I carried on: *When the enterprising burglar's not a-burgling (not a-burgling) when the cut-throat isn't occupied in crime ('pied in crime) 'e loves to 'ear the little brook a-gurgling (brook a-gurgling) and listen to the merry village chime. When the 'coster's finished jumping on his mother, 'e likes to lie a basking in the sun (in the sun). Ah take one consideration with another (with another) a policeman's lot is not a 'appy one.*

Nick joined me for: *When constabulary duties to be done, to be done, a policeman's lot is not a 'appy one --- ('appy one)!*

MMM: He's tried to get me to sing Three Little Maids From School Are We. He doesn't seem to realize that

Japanese do not consider the Mikado to be oriental in any way, not even in the costumes. But sometimes I please my Lord and Master with a *One little maid is bride, Yum Yum, two little maids in attendance come, three little maids is the total sum, three little maids from school.*

A while back in the 60s I tried to write some lyrics for the civil rights marches using that Policemen's Lot song with modern words, but it didn't work. Of course I lack William Gilbert's wit and vocabulary, but even so I was too passionate about the cause to make light of the policemen's predicament in beating us down.

Jennings took my knowledge of song lyrics to inquire if I was gay.

"Jesus H. Gonzales!" I exploded. "Not this lifetime! Can't a feller remember intelligent songs and still be partial to women?"

I overdid it with the umbrage. It turned out that Jennings is gay. Nick jumped into the fray.

"You see? That's the very reason for this fishing trip. We needed this meeting to know more about our attitudes and issues. We need to get better acquainted."

"So, do you have friends who are in fact police officers?" Jennings asked. That is a standard question for prospective jurors I've learned. They are weeded out from serving in our courts under the fear they might unfairly favor prosecutions. That doesn't seem like a good idea to me.

"I have one friend who is employed by the Sheriff's Department to manage incarcerated youth mostly in camps up in the mountains. He has some kind of a badge. We have not discussed how liberal either of us are. He's a white fellow with a strong southern accent and I wouldn't trust him to know about some of the ideas in my head, such as equal rights for all."

Actually, he's only my friend because our wives are friends but I didn't feel that was necessary information for Jennings. No need to be defensive.

> MMM: Yes, I know the fellow. They only meet and talk when we are four together, never by themselves.

I gave Jennings a little talk about my feelings. I have no quarrel with police who arrest demonstrators for trampling on public flower beds or green lawns, for littering, or for loitering, or for violation of traffic laws or such. Let them give citations or arrest us for violating the law. But for some reason our police forces have often served the interests of rich property owners and not in protecting the constitutional rights of citizens who have been trampled on by those property owners. They've allowed themselves to be seen as thugs in the employ of plutocrats and not in service of the average citizen.

To hear an officer with a loud speaker declare 'This is an unlawful assembly, disperse or be arrested!' smacks me of dictatorships and abuse of power. Especially if the police are on horseback. That reminds me of the Russian Revolution with Cossacks wielding sabers, and rifles breaking up the demonstrations against the Tsar. (Doctor Zhivago!)

Thanks to television we've seen dozens of newsreels of such events in foreign dictatorships. Use of dogs or fire hoses on peaceful demonstrators in this country should not be tolerated, but they were used here in the sixties to our everlasting shame.

I had an aunt once who commented about the Freedom Riders in the 50s who were beaten up just for boarding buses in a mixed group of blacks and whites, "Why are those people causing trouble?"

I couldn't believe the question. Friends who happen to be Aryan and Non-Aryan cause trouble by boarding a public bus and sitting together, in the twentieth century? I would like to suggest that the persons taking them off the bus and beating upon their persons with axe handles or baseball bats are the ones causing trouble.

Some blame attaches to liberals or the undercover provocateurs who shout pigs! or other insults at the authorities. Incivility damages our righteous cause. The moral high ground gets clouded. We need to realize that provocateurs from either side may be among us with a different agenda, but true liberals should never join in shouting insults at any public safety officers.

Back in 1948 Harry Truman made a whistle stop campaign tour, speaking from the back of a train at towns along the way to crowds that had heard of his schedule. Our class teacher took us to the station to see the President. The police struggled to hold back students and citizens who only wanted a personal glimpse of the President behind some ropes as people pushed to get closer to the train.

Two wise guys from my class were insult artists. One shouted, "Hey, Jack, does your dad work?" And the other shouted back, "Naw, he's a cop!" That shocked me at the time but of course our public discourse has sunk even further downhill since then.

We liberals need to celebrate law and order. Of course law and order makes fascism possible, but it also makes liberty possible. Anarchy is no friend of liberty. It contains extreme evil as much as fascism contains extreme evil. Both are power run amuck. Think of the French Revolution and the guillotine's victims.

The famous saying: 'Power corrupts and absolute power corrupts absolutely' is beautiful if we understand that it includes power in the hands of monarchists or republicans, law and order or anarchists, left or right or center, deists or atheists. All true believers are equally susceptible to corruption.

Perhaps that idea of omnipotence in one party's hands was anathema to God Himself, and that is why he created Free Will and allowed the Satanic revolt to sort things out. I expect any day now to read a letter to the editor of the Times defending the revolt of Satan and his minions due to unfair favoritism and lack of appreciation for their contribution to the universe. The editors must print both sides of every issue! Jesus H. Martinez! It makes my blood boil to even imagine it, let alone actually read it!

We need to support normal police work and overlook the occasional shooting or beating or jailing of an innocent person. Accidents happen. Punishing mistakes made by professionals such as doctors or law enforcers by transferring large sums of money from the taxpayers to the benefit of the injured parties takes energy and resources away from overall public protection.

It seems to me that well armed barbarians are making war on civilization and need to be confronted with deadly force. Can we have a defensive war on our streets without innocent lives being lost? We need a lid on the license to kill but still we need to authorize that license. The threat of deadly force should be a deterrent to lawbreakers.

As it is now, an armed robber figures he can easily outrun police who carry guns but have no authorization to use them, except in clear situations of self defense. That stinks. I'm getting sick of those scenes in the movies where Dirty Harry or other policemen must chase on foot the bad guys for long periods across the streets of traffic and from rooftops to rooftops. What a boring idea for action. Must we endure obligatory foot race scenes in every movie with cops and robbers? It's getting old. If it mimics true police work, we need to find better methods of detaining suspects.

The same situation exists with lawbreakers in vehicles running from the law. There are actually people who write letters to the editor stating that lawbreakers should not be pursued at high speed because innocent persons or property could be harmed if they get in the way of either party. Huh? These people must be egocentric comedians, certainly not serious thinkers.

All of us should have some fear of our peace officers dressed in blue/black uniforms with pistols on their belt. We need to stop and answer questions. The police shouldn't have to follow fleeing suspects without firing a shot across their front. If a shout or a siren doesn't halt the suspect then a loud gunshot should give them pause. If the bullet causes some injury or damage that was not intended the fault lies with the fleeing suspect and any recompense should come from them, not the police department and not the public purse.

I saw a foreign movie where the first shell in the police pistol is a blank. The noise of the first shot is to get attention without causing damage. But everyone needs to understand the second shot can be deadly.

Jennings agreed and said, "This idea that the public should pay millions of dollars for accidental damage from our law enforcers is nonsense. Somebody decided that damage caused by a felon isn't recoverable because felons rarely have deep pockets. Society may wish to reimburse the innocent for their damages but somehow the lawyers have decided that millions of dollars should also be taken from the taxpayers for the temerity of hiring persons capable of making a mistake. The millions added to the actual costs are to send a message that the police need to be reined in from making mistakes. Sorry, I get the wrong message from that because the lawyers get most of message money, don't they?"

We both felt the same way about capital punishment. It should be on the books, but we should be ashamed about the way it is used. We've tinkered too much trying for a goal of perfection that is not possible in this world of free will.

Jennings said he's on an inter-chapter steering committee for the ACLU, and had heard my name, but never seen me at any meetings. I admitted it.

"It's been a year since I've been active there."

"Less interested in defending the constitution?"

"No, it's just that I wasn't comfortable the last three or four meetings. I'll come out with it. I thought it was a mistake to organize chapters on special interests, for example, a Gay Chapter."

"Oops."

"I think it goes outside the box the ACLU was founded on. We were organized to defend the Bill of Rights, not advance social issues. Having chapters based on geographical areas seems to be a better way of having neutral ideas about issues, puts focus strictly on the constitution. Our focus needs to be on that basis only, rights of citizens being ignored or trampled by government agencies.

I can never find the persuasive words to suggest passion should be intellectual and not visceral at least in legal matters. That's probably because my own passion is more visceral and not intellectual.

What I meant was: Sure, the Gay Chapter can provide support for the court tests to secure the rights of gays to exist openly in society. I was stunned when I discovered the police actually arrested persons just for being gay. Gay behavior was against the law! The police went into gay bars with nightsticks and flailed the patrons without mercy.

In the 1950s I read in the papers of police officers peeking through the window of a known prostitute to see if she was entertaining male visitors within her own home. The crime was called resorting. We give the police power to keep our streets free of such commerce but it seems to me that peeking through a citizen's windows is not tolerable.

Come to think of it, there is a famous case where the police peeked through the window of a married couple in Virginia and then invaded their home to arrest them for resorting because their marriage license was invalid in Virginia. That southern state refused to acknowledge marriage between males and females of certain ethnic origins. They defined separate races as: white, black, red, yellow, and Malay! Malay? Look it up. It has a capital letter in their law, lower case in the other four categories.

Bryan had an answer for that but I think we've put enough sunshine on that conversation. For what it's worth I believe the representatives from the Gay Men's ACLU chapter always put the rest of the chapters to shame.

They have the fastest growing membership, always attend meetings with well groomed neat appearance in suits and ties, have their agenda printed ahead of time and move the meetings along effectively. We haven't had such terrific clean cut members since the FBI gave up infiltrating us and paying dues. Didn't they?

There is a long list of possibly gay persons that I admire tremendously for their talent, intellect, and contributions to civilization but I don't need to know about their private inclinations. It's not important to me. To me Liberace is a great showman and decent pianist. I don't wonder about his private life. That's why we call it private. Men should be allowed to be flamboyant and effeminate if they want without being accused of unusual bedroom activities.

For example just as I don't want to know about my parents, or George and Martha or Abraham and Mary in bed I don't need to know about anyone's proclivities in their own bedrooms. It's not on the table. Don't tell me about it. It's not a fit topic for speculation. Homo or hetero is just normal life in our species. I believe in four orientations: hetero, homo, bi-sexual and nonsexual. Nature created it, accept it. Forget about it.

Not to put too fine a point on it, but the cases of Julius Caesar and Eleanor Roosevelt come to mind. I believe when Shakespeare uses the term 'thy lover' by some soothsayer guy in the street who tries to warn the general about a coup, the word 'lover' means 'admirer.'

When Mrs. Roosevelt wrote what pass for love letters to a lady friend, it's just that she was prone to effusive gushing on paper, being denied tender physical affection in her fishbowl life, especially with such a merciless, bloodless mother-in-law. Written notes with tender flatteries are no proof of a carnal sex life. The perpetrators of such rumors are either touting forgeries for money or fame or they are persons with too much dirty imagination.

As much as I despise J. Edgar Hoover for his harassment of Dr. King as well as other misuses of power I refuse to join in the cheap shots at him since he died. So what if he did wear a dress to a party? So what if he did share a life or a living arrangement with another man? What executive hasn't put on a dress or makeup to entertain his troops at a party, and there are such persons as non-sexual. People should not assume facts not in evidence. Especially media people such as comedians using rumors or suspicions for a cheap laugh.

I came by this way of thinking from a class in police science that I took in college. It was to sort through words to find actual verifiable evidence. For example in the stage play Twelve Angry Men, there is this dialog statement: The old man saw the knifing. Saw the boy kill his father!

The words -- saw – kill -- are not sufficient evidence on its face to establish murder. First we'd need to know if death occurred by loss of blood from a knife wound. Perhaps the knife may have been brandished but not inserted. More details might establish credibility but just for a person to say he witnessed murder from a distance is not conclusive evidence. Especially if that witness was not wearing their corrective lenses, if it was at night at some distance from the scene. It may be suggestive but not conclusive.

My class in Police Science was called General Semantics 101 and the texts were from S.I. Hayakawa and Count Alfred Korzybski. I might also quote the Bible where it requires two witnesses to condemn another person of murder.

Jennings came to life when I mentioned Dr. Hayakawa. Jennings said, "Our language controls our emotions and actions. As long as we keep saying Lincoln freed the slaves, we'll never persuade the white South that he was a great man. Any decent man should free slaves. That shouldn't be enough to qualify one for sainthood. When we say Lincoln freed the children of captured Africans from degrading bondage similar to the Hebrews in Egypt, then everyone can appreciate the wisdom and humanity involved."

I got it, but Nick did not. He didn't think Lincoln's reputation needed any more burnishing. He still had the mind set that slaves were commodities to be bought, sold, bred, or freed. He thinks it was just the economic stroke of losing their property that made the white masters angry and abusive. It's OK. He's still a liberal.

I offered my own take on it: the Caucasian people of the South used to live close to their enslaved servants. When the law changed, making those servants human beings like the masters, the masters could not accept that they had been evildoers or that slavery is evil. It had to be God's Will that persons minding their own business in Africa had to become servants and field workers of persons born in Europe. It was Cain's penalty perhaps. Can you believe it? They did. Some still do.

There was another reason for my lack of attendance at ACLU headquarters this year. At the last steering committee I participated in there was a competition among all the chapter representatives to be the most liberal. For instance I might go along with the government having to prove a person without documentation is a foreigner to be deported, but gave up when the writers framing the argument insisted that the undocumented person is entitled to a court appointed and reimbursed lawyer to fight deportation.

To their way of thinking anyone arriving within our borders is immediately entitled to court hearings at taxpayer expense to prevent being expelled from the country. Oh, please! I think it was mob psychology and a competition to see who could be more liberal than the person next to them. That stinks.

Nick sensed some strong negative vibes between Bryan and me. He raised a fist in a demonstrator mode and sang a cappella a couple of freedom rider lines that I remembered from the late 50s. I can't remember the last name of the composer but his first name was Jerry.

> *(singing) You're only hurting your cause this way*
> *That's what all of us liberals say*
> *No one likes things the way they are*
> *But you go too fast and you go too far*

From what I've written you may be thinking Nick and Warren are more liberal than I am. I happen to think they've gone down a blind side alley and I'm unable to describe how I arrived at this conclusion without dishonoring myself. So I will.

> MMM: Again my husband has gone off the deep end, speculating about immoral pseudo justifications for self gratifying desires. It serves no purpose to denounce two citizens in this manuscript that he disagreed with. I've deleted a long harangue that he rightfully judged 'dishonored himself.'

We found their favorite fishing spot and dropped our lines into the blue to see what was hungry. I was lucky, not even a nibble.

Chapter Six

August

There was one more fellow I should mention who was involved in the Nick Cufflett milieu. Shortly after the fishing trip I received a phone call from a Lal Patel. He knew me from some activist group we'd both been involved with. I think it was Greenpeace or Save the Whales, or it could have been the more militant Sea Shepherd. He wanted to meet with me for some confidential discussion. I agreed to meet him at an Indian curry place on Pioneer Boulevard in Artesia.

Even though he's a native born American he and I are not communicating smoothly and I don't know why that is. For example, we met in a night school class years ago and I made the clumsy mistake of taking him for an expert in the culture of India. At least my thinking was that he was closer to it and could explain some of it.

I'll confess here to a lack of respect on my part for India with its sacred cows, pantheon of deities, and overpopulation. But my first question to Lal was about the caste system there. I knew about Brahmins and Untouchables vaguely. In my fictional reading of British novels they sometimes mentioned a half-caste girl who marries the trading company's executive officer's son. I also wondered what caste it would be for the child of a Brahmin and an Untouchable. But that was just idle curiosity. Let's assume it would be Untouchable.

If I had been born rich instead of so breathtakingly intelligent I would own a copy of the Oxford English Dictionary. I would be able to look up (I hope) half-caste and see the first usage in print and how it describes the term. That is, if hyphenated words or phrases are in the OED. I have great respect for public libraries that have a copy of the OED opened on a reading stand for easy access.

For some reason both Brits and Indians have a class system but we tend to think of the Indians as being more rigid. Did our forefounders leave Great Britain partly because of class consciousness? Now that I think about it, is the caste system in India only for Hindus? What is the social standing of a Muslim in an Indian environment then?

I take the blame for the awkward communication between Lal and myself. I forget the exact wording now, but I put the question badly. His answer was from the viewpoint of a California born person of Indian descent so it probably isn't for attribution and I should not mangle it here. But sometimes I think I was put on this earth to mangle and tangle and sort out baffling puzzles.

His answer, if I may paraphrase and interpret freely was: a person rises through the caste system (I knew that already) but the use of the word half-caste was a British euphemism for intermarriage of Europeans with Sub-Continentals. And in his opinion it is a racist term in the west, suggesting the person's social standing has a cloud on it. It has no relationship to the original concept of castes in India, unless it is to suggest the existence of a new caste, the half-breed.

He then dismissed the topic by throwing into the mix a new topic -- the half-breed. Now that there are so many people traveling the world and intermarrying there are exotic genetics involved.

His thoughts may have been leading somewhere but I jumped in with my ideas about yellow fever – where some Caucasians, especially males, find the girls in the Orient to be irresistibly desirable.

MMM: Oh, no! Not again! Let me out of here!

Lal countered with an explanation that involves transmigration of souls, reincarnation. He said he was ready to believe that one's soul has no caste as his ancestors believed. While it was possible in the old days to define persons according to certain occupations and traditions, intermarriage has trashed that concept. Few of us in the western world, at least, know our corporeal or spiritual pedigrees. He was happy to embrace the concept that souls are only seeking wisdom from the universe and that Brahmins are not the end of that search for broader experiences.

Our discussion got into civil rights at that point. It became more an issue to me that one's race, although traceable genetically, cannot be traced in the higher self, which is the soul. Souls lack identification with earth geography. Souls are more important than our bodies. Bodies of mixed so-called races may look exotic but that is a very superficial assessment. It is the soul's pedigree, its accumulated wisdom and experience that is important.

"You know, of course," Lal said, "that His Holiness the Dalai Lama is the spiritual leader of Tibet, due to the pedigree of his soul, and yet his biological parents are ethnic Chinese and he was discovered as a child living outside the modern boundaries of Tibet -- not in the Portola where the thirteenth Dalai Lama died."

"Of course," I replied. "Mitsi and I heard him speak at the Claremont Colleges. I purchased a souvenir T-Shirt that said Hello Dalai for my brother. And of course, I read his My Land and My People."

Actually, I'd been tuned into the Dalai Lama since high school when his picture graced the cover of a Time magazine. He was a teen-ager like myself with the same crewcut and wearing glasses like mine. We looked a little alike. But I was a humble student and he was a demi-god.

I was serving in the marines when the newspapers described his escape from the Chinese Army's invasion of the Portola. I was in suspense for weeks after he disappeared into mountain fogs on horseback and reappeared across the border in India.

That feat confirmed some divine intervention in my book. It seemed to me that from his life story we could speculate that souls do migrate across ethnic lines rather than stay within one family or one tribe.

The famous speech by Dr. Martin Luther King Jr. about the content of our character is more important than the content in our skin said it better. Needless to say his exact words said it better than what I've paraphrased. My conclusion was that souls do not reflect the racial characteristics that define our bodies.

Somewhere back in the memory of books read I think James Michener touched on this in his novel Hawaii. Although I don't remember him using the concept of soul he did introduce the concept of mankind composed of men with golden skin, from intermarriage over generations. He had a wife with Japanese ancestry, you know.

Lal has a mustache and is about forty years old. I didn't know him back in the days of the Nehru jacket fad but in my imagination he was often so attired. These days he wore casual clothes, a retro 50s look, mostly Hawaiian shirts with blue denim trousers. He lacks the Indian accent where they constrict the throat and speak in a higher pitch than we do.

As I said previously Lal was born here in California. I was at his wedding to a voluptuous girl named Surendar. I don't usually think of girls from that part of the world as voluptuous or zaftig, but she was very. She was very, very memorable and not just for the well chosen name.

After the greeting and ordering of some light fare he got down to business. He knew Nick Cufflett and seemed to be aware that Nick and I had met more than once this summer. He said that Nick seemed to be recruiting prospective individuals and he had been interviewed, wondered if I had also been surveyed.

"Yes," I answered. "I suppose I've been interviewed indirectly. Nick wanted to get to know my personally and I put some distance between us."

"Aha!" Lal smiled. "Then I'm wasting my time, if you'll forgive me for saying that time with you is wasteful."

I was taken aback and replied, "Oh, I can understand the wording of that comment. I don't take it personally."

"I was curious about Mr. Cufflett. He seems to be a business tycoon who wishes to hang out with us peons."

"Another curious choice of words," I said, starting to take offense. Although in the big picture, Lal was quite correct. He and I were not fixed for life as Nick seemed to be.

"I finally discovered Mr. Cufflett's purpose in joining so many liberal issues oriented groups."

"Don't keep me in suspense," I replied as Lal became occupied with his tea, studying its color and heat.

"He's got money and now he wants power. He wants to be a Governor or U.S. Senator from the State of California. He's beating the bushes for grassroots supporters. He's looking for experienced hardcore cadres with membership names and addresses."

This was a startling idea to me. For some, unstated reason, I had discounted Nick's claim to be from Chicago. He had often used Canadian vernacular pronunciations. I therefore had assumed Nick Cufflett was Canadian. Then of course it occurred to me that Canadians become

U.S. citizens. And I could think of a couple of Congressmen who were naturalized American citizens.

Hardcore cadres? Again Lal was choosing interesting words that provoked curiosity about his underlying definitions. I had never considered political ambition in Nick Cufflett. Perhaps I'd overlooked it due to ego as Lal was now pointing out. I thought Nick had been cultivating me for my manly persona and intellectual conversation. Now that Lal put it in perspective, it was obvious.

Lal had another arrow to aim at Nick's reputation. He said, "Have you ever seen the family name Cufflett in the phone book?"

I admitted that I hadn't. He went on to say that Cufflett was a truncated piece of an Italian family name, something like Cuffletti. I countered with "I think he is Jewish, not Italian."

"The two are not mutually exclusive," Lal replied. "One does not have to be Catholic to be Italian."

I instantly agreed with him and felt shame at my statement. "I see said the blind man as he picked up his hammer and saw." Of course Cufflett could be a Canadian born Jew from Italian immigrants to the Great White North who moved to Chicago before he became an adult. It has become that kind of world!

In my mind I was formulating a reply admitting details of the meetings with Nick and our topics of conversation. I might have put them into words if Lal had not been too obvious in cross examining me about those meetings.

My close mouth antennae went up when Lal said Nick has some questionable background, especially regarding his source of wealth.

"So, you are more cautious than you look," Lal said, again ticking me off with his choice of language.

"We never really got into any direct offers or declining of offers. We spoke about our feelings on issues and it seems he's more liberal than I am willing to admit to."

"Oh, you only talked politics?"

"What else is there?"

"With me it was business. He openly asked me if Patel was a very common name, or if many of the Patels in business in California were related."

From here on I'm going to paraphrase his story. I said, "I guess I was wrong about Cufflett. I probably blew my chance for monetary gain. How many chances do we get?"

> MMM: Sorry, he's gone off on that same topic again. Defamation of a VIP's intentions according to his own hunches by way of hearsay evidence from Mr. Patel. I've deleted both of their exchanges.

Wrong tack. Lal went ballistic while seated at the table in the Hello Delhi's Kitchen. His eyes got wide and he gesticulated by throwing his arms and hands in end-of-the-world panic.

When he calmed down and wiped his mouth with a napkin he said, "I understood that you said you put space between you and Cufflett. I tell you something bad about him and now you actually regret not joining him for ill gotten wealth, of becoming a tool of someone who is dishonest?"

"You haven't said Cufflett is dishonest. I just imagine he and I are not on the same moral page. Business can be painted as bullies vs. the little guy, but that is nature, not morality. It's natural for the strong to grow stronger and the weak to get weaker."

Lal answered with, "I didn't know I had to furnish details in describing my beef with Cufflett." He actually used the word beef. I guess the word is all right to use, as long as he never ingests beef itself, assuming that he's following his ancestral proclivities.

"In phone calls that I made to fellow Patels it seems many of them knew Cufflett's reputation in the monetary sense.

> MMM: Again I've deleted hearsay rumors impugning Mr. Cufflett's reputation

That put an entirely new light on Cufflett. Accusations can be false or inaccurate. We have no way of knowing what promises he made in return for thousands of dollars. Still, I would prefer to err on the side of honesty and decency and forget about reconciling whatever connection I had with Cufflett.

But Lal was not sure I had joined his camp. He came up with another damaging broadside attack. He said, "In my phone calls with fellow Patels, one of them who was not a burned investor recognized the name anyway. He said that when he lived on the East Coast he heard about a Cuffletti family that controlled a pizza cheese cartel. Pizza parlors who insisted on using their own unprocessed cheese would experience intensive price competitions or unusual bad luck of some kind.

> MMM: Again, I deleted a few hundred words suggesting a scurrilous connection to our Mr. Cufflett, not being content with Jay's next paragraph.

The name Cufflett and Cuffletti is strictly hearsay innuendo, and nothing to be held against someone. No, Lal had a little more dirt to throw but I have thrown in the towel. No need for me to spell it out here. It's not verifiable. Just consider me out.

In a spirit of friendship Lal and I continued our conversation about non-Cufflett issues. I wasn't careful enough to avoid the issue of religion, though. Don't get Lal started on religion. He insists his ancestors invented religion and the pantheon concept of gods, and none of the upstart religions that have proceeded onto the world stage since can eclipse them.

I said, "I can't get behind the idea of animalistic headed gods, though. Um, like the Egyptians with their human bodies having a bird's head, for example."

Lal responded with, "But you think nothing about graphic novels today where human beings wear bird masks, such as the superhero, Hawk Man. What about Batman? The gods were superheroes in the old days with extraordinary powers and visages. None are real, of course. Neither the Egyptian gods nor the comic book heroes. Let's not waste time discussing fiction."

We both have a mutual respect for the great Mahatma, Mohandas K. Gandhi. Gandhi was a difficult leader to pin into one religion. He seemed religious in a wider sense than just one discipline. Someone asked him, what do you think of Christianity and he replied, "I think it would be a good idea."

I've told Mitsi that if I should expire before her, I hope my last words will be the same as Gandhi's, "Oh God!" when he was shot.

I've since found better last words, though, in Joseph Conrad's Heart of Darkness. The phrase was in two places in the novel. In Apocalypse Now, Marlon Brando's Colonel Kurtz says, "the horror --- the horror ---" Now I want my recorded last words to be "the honeys --- the honeys ---"

MMM: Duly noted.

I asked Lal if he believed in an after life. He answered, "Of course. You and I are as we speak living an actual after life. We lived before in many incarnations and we will live again after this present incarnation."

Lal continued: This is heaven, this is hell, this is an after life for all of us The truth has always been in front of our noses and yet we look up at the heavens or into the bowels of the earth for non-existent destinations for our souls. We are designed for the earth and will inhabit the earth forever or however long that turns out to be.

I said, "Are you suggesting I can be my own Grandpa?" He replied, "Yes, if your Grandpa's body died before you were born, you could be reincarnated into the same family. Possibly.

I should have discussed it further, but my mind went into a hillbilly ditty called "I'm my own Grandpa" and that lyric involved incestuous marriages and attempts to present an insoluble riddle that was based on legal documents, not blood or souls.

Now I remembered why I kept in touch with Patel in addition to our shared interest in the whales. He spoke authoritatively about philosophy in words or concepts that I could almost understand. That may be the reason we have so many gurus making disciples here in the U.S. They use a language we can access.

Those German philosophers use terms and ideas I can't get into. Woody Allen, who seems to have studied them suggests all deep discussions must begin with 'let's define our terms.' That is a side issue that leads into blind alleys with me.

Patel said (paraphrasing here) we all know the earth is composed of animals, plants, and minerals. Plants and animals return to minerals which are the building blocks of life. Dead animals, including insects, enrich the mineral soil to grow new plants to be eaten by animals, and then again become minerals. The circle of life includes minerals according to Lal.

In my head I interpreted the introduction of plants and animals as the breath of God after He fashioned Adam out of clay.

I reflected about the human body being composed of minerals/ chemicals – water, calcium, and other inert materials. Both plants and animals somehow transmute those minerals to serve our life activities, and in the end we return those minerals to the earth for recycling. Dust to dust.

I once received a letter from my friend, Alvanez, in the Philippines saying that a typhoon had devastated a wide area in those islands, but his area was protected from the furious winds by its nearby volcano. He's too sophisticated to attribute his area's salvation to divine intervention, but if other local people say the god of their volcano defeated the god of the typhoons, the language does not negate the facts of the event.

I mentally affirmed my wish to be cremated. And it made sense that Gandhi and Nehru's bodies were cremated and scattered in the Ganges. The earth recycles everything, from the humblest among us to the greatest among us. All we can do is ease the process.

After we parted ways I purchased a package of tea from India. As I got into my car I sang to myself, *"So Long Oolong, How Long You Gonna Be Gone?"* Ah, the good old songs.

Chapter Seven

September

Mitsi and I took a quick vacation in Vancouver, British Columbia before her classes started again at the university. We heard rumors that many Hong Kong chinese were buying into Vancouver. The terrain seems familiar to them with the large island just offshore accessible by ferryboats. They tend to prefer a British flag and British culture, even if it is a Maple Leaf instead of the Union Jack. It still isn't the Communist red flag of anarchy and revolution.

Poor souls. Little do they suspect how rampant the French culture is in Canada. Every package, every sign, must be in two languages. I wonder if they actually come in by the millions if there will some day be three languages on packages and signs.

When we returned to good old 401 Susan called to say that she had been to Las Vegas with Tom and SHE. She said Tom took rejection stoically. He quoted Frankie Laine's song, The Moonlight Gambler, saying *If you've never gambled on love and lost then you haven't gambled at all.*

He was more heartbroken, though, when SHE moved out of their apartment without giving any of us a forwarding address. A note she left said she didn't want to be a burden on Susan, Tom, or Jay any longer.

A phone call wouldn't do it for me. I had to go over to Sakura Gardens to commiserate in person. Susan showed me the closet where her visitor's clothes and personal items had been. She had left behind a few things including some souvenirs purchased in Las Vegas.

I said, "Did she gamble at all? Maybe she won a jackpot and wanted to keep it a secret and---"

"No, she didn't even try the slots with the quarter you gave her."

"Dang!"

"Have you and SHE received any nibbles about any of those millionaires you were hoping to match up with? Maybe she---"

"No, I was her contact with the agencies, and I would have known if anyone was interested. There really hasn't been enough time. I'm sure she would have gotten some matches to consider."

"Now that I think about it, wasn't she just a little bit too perfect, too -- perfect? Could she have been a North Korean or Communist Chinese spy sent here to infiltrate the country obliquely, to become a mole? She wouldn't be suspected until---"

"Wow! You should write a novel, Jay!"

> MMM: I considered moving those last two paragraphs down to the very end, the very last words.

"She could be very effective over on the east coast, among the movers and shakers and politically powerful. I can imagine her at diplomatic soirees."

I envisioned her at a beltway party, sipping champagne, surrounded by diplomats and military field marshals. Or was I just recalling a long ago story I read about Mata Hari? I do tend to even recycle thoughts, it seems.

I have not yet written any novels but I bit my tongue rather than remind Susan about my screenplay, The Falls. It begins with a prepilgrim native princess now known as The Maid of the Mist sacrificed by her tribe to appease the Niagara River gods. Since meeting SHE I realized that she would be perfect for that role, if my work was ever to be filmed.

The story goes from her paddling a canoe over the falls into a modern day remake of the Marilyn Monroe-Joseph Cotten story from the 1950s, of a young wife, married to an older man, with a young lover. I had poured my soul into that Maid of the Mist prologue, and she appears again in the modern story as the director's chief assistant, as we see the pre-production team scouting shots at Niagara for their version of the screenplay. A couple of years ago I shared it with Susan for her input, and she trashed the Maid of the Mist story as historically inaccurate, politically incorrect and insulting to the Canadian and U. S. citizens of indigenous descent.

My intention with the visit was to offer to treat Susan to a supper somewhere. When I broached the subject she took it as a signal that I was hungry, myself. She opened her refrigerator door and indicated I should look around on the shelves.

She had a case of imported French drinking water. I've drunk store bought water all my adult life, but never imported from out of the country. When you think about it, our bodies are mostly water. If Susan drank nothing but French water probably ninety percent of her body was from France. In that case she should be eligible for French citizenship, *n'est pas?*

She said, "I can offer you a coke and a cheese sandwich."

"Best offer I've had today," I replied.

She didn't put any mayonnaise or mustard on the bread but I ate it anyway. I could see her mayonnaise was not my Miracle Whip brand,

and her mustard was not French's Yellow. (Product placement pending) Biting into this cheese sandwich I suddenly remembered I hadn't had a BLC in years.

They should be more popular than BLTs at coffee shops --bacon, lettuce, and cheese with Miracle Whip. Maybe they were my mother's specialty and not anyone else's. I couldn't ask Mitsi to go to all that trouble, preparing slices of bacon for my sandwiches, something only a mother would do, but that sure makes a good sandwich.

I brought with me a one page idea for Susan to pursue if she wishes. I gave up on it but with her knowledge of science she could be successful in creating a television series for the networks, or a public cable company. Mitsi has been reading mystery books, and we shopped at the Mystery Book Store where we found several books by Isaac Asimov.

Asimov in real life belongs to a men's club called the Trapdoor Spiders. They meet once a month to discuss riddles or weighty ideas and different members of the club gain or provide expertise.

He wrote several books that fictionalizes his group and he called them The Black Widowers. The first book in his series that Mitsi read was Banquets of the Black Widowers. She and I had some discussions about the riddles the members discussed and when I noticed that the waiter who serves the dinner always has the last word it struck me as a perfect half hour television show with good intellectual conversation and analysis.

I previously stated that I'm a big fan of the stage play Twelve Angry Men. Asimov's men were not angry, but they came from disparate disciplines as a jury to find the most reasonable solution to a question on a regular basis.

I gave Susan a sheet of paper with the idea sketched and she said it sounds interesting.

****

Script for a half hour television program to develop as producer-writer:
ISAAC ASIMOV'S BANQUETS OF THE BLACK WIDOWERS.

Each episode takes place in an upscale banquet room, perhaps a luxury
hotel with a marquee board listing the group, room, and time for the
dinner. Possible tie-in to cover some production costs.

The club members have eminent credentials and credibility. The artist
(thinking Jose Ferrer) dresses flamboyantly and receives banter from
the others as they arrive, often critical. He usually sketches while the
discussions proceed and may or may not offer a sketch of how he would
solve the riddle. Another character orders a special drink each time on
arrival. Often the characters discuss the menu and the specialties of the
evening. The characters may include a police inspector, a medical doctor,
research chemists, astronomers, linguists, psychologists---

They are presented with a puzzle by the host, a rotating role for each
member to arrange the place, food, and program. After suggesting various
solutions that none of them can agree on, the waiter, Jackson, offers his
idea, which is immediately grasped as the obvious one after hearing it.
He modestly suggests that the others have cleared away the extraneous
details and he arrived at his opinion via the process of elimination.

There should be continuing characters with guest members from time
to time. A pilot script from one of Asimov's short stories has a guest with
a newlywed problem: his bride, with bright red hair, claims that she is a
witch. She has demonstrated supernatural powers such as disappearing
and reappearing elsewhere. He wishes the Black Widowers can suggest
rational explanations for a recent event at a restaurant.

These situations for discussion and resolutions may be presented as
short films. The guest may narrate silent visual scenes, presenting the
riddle.

****

I also gave her two of the Isaac Asimov books that we had bought at the Mystery Book Shop. After a few more moments of chit chat, some inquiries about Mitsi and what plans we had upcoming, I said, "Well, I should go pay my respects to Tom, if he's in."

"I told him you were coming over. I think he's anxious to see you."

I finished up the snack by downing the coke and rinsing the bottle at the sink. I always rinse bottles and cans before discarding or putting them in a recycling bin. I thanked Susan for her usual hospitality and left.

The lights were on in Tom's quarters so I knocked and he came downstairs to let me in. Awhile back I opined that I might have made a good diplomat. When I met with Tom I told him that I had painted him in the best possible light with SHE. I told him that I considered his profession, gardening, to be the noblest effort on earth, anointed and sanctified by God in the Garden of Eden.

God may have intended us to be his eyes and ears on this sphere and his agent to help maintain equilibrium. For example mankind might have been created specifically to assist whales find relief from those pesky barnacles and some day mankind will find a cure. Until that day they must leap and breach to dislodge some of the irritating creatures.

That is my spin from Kurt Vonnegut Jr. in The Sirens of Titan where space travelers stranded there somehow have to wait for evolution and mankind to inadvertently manufacture a particular small but important piece of metal they can use to repair their transport ship.

Tom nodded appreciation when I suggested that my powers of persuasion were not the best but had been delivered in earnest.

"I was hit with a double whammy, Jay. I lost a thousand dollars at blackjack so I'm a two time loser on that trip," he said in an effort to downplay his broken heart, equating it with a thousand dollars.

"I should have known better than to go into the tables with a negative aura. It was a stupid move on my part. I quit the tables when I realized that."

I avoided mentioning SHE. "How was the new car? Did it handle well on Route 15 through the passes?"

"It was made for that kind of driving," he answered. "SHE drove at a steady 70 mph and kept a vigilant eye at all times for traffic in front and behind. She's very careful not to hit the brakes suddenly or hard. She always keeps a decent interval behind the cars ahead.

"I suppose this was her first trip to another state."

"Yeah, she noticed when we were ten to fifteen miles from the state line that the topography was all different. California is not a natural extension of Nevada. I explained to her that California was probably once an island that bumped into the mainland. There are some geologists that predict an earthquake will separate California from Nevada and it will go back to being a Pacific island again."

"What about her first impression of Las Vegas. She had to be impressed, right?"

"I had it timed perfectly. I took over the driving after we stopped at the state line for gas. We got there about eight at night. The lights of the place were dazzling even for me, and I had been there before. Each time I go the colors and lights are more elaborate!

We checked into Caesar's, and got adjacent rooms, one for the girls and one for me. We took quick showers and dressed for dinner. SHE wore a little black cocktail dress like I didn't know you could find in Santa Monica. It stupefied me.

She was wide eyed and amazed at the luxury and lights and atmosphere. She stood and looked a long time at Cleopatra's Barge. People walking past looked back at her rather than at the barge. And at the statue of David she said, 'Did they buy that from Italy? I never imagined it was so big!'

Aw, man, you should have seen her walk through the casino. She has a wonderful walk, sort of a casual mosey that is just so elegant. And you know how she has this really sexy voice, soft, musical and accented. There's terrific enchantment in her aura and everywhere we went people noticed her. I was very proud."

"I'll bet," I said.

"And you should have seen how the diehard Vegas gamblers who can ignore fire and earthquakes could not ignore her. They took their eyes off the tables or slots for a moment or two, as if hypnotized."

I could imagine. Now I was beginning to regret not going with them. Maybe with the four of us walking through a casino people would -- no, they'd assume Susan was with me and Tom was the stud.

Tom went on to suggest that he couldn't help wishing to have it all. He used my patent worthy phrase -- 'I almost had it, but it turned out to be just out of reach. Just out of reach'.

Looking back I can see many unfinished reaches in my own life. In Scouts I only reached Life Scout. Didn't even try for the top rank of Eagle. In the university I stopped at Master's. Didn't even try for Ph D. In judo, I didn't even reach for Brown Belt, let alone attain the Black Belt.

I've persuaded myself that I am a dabbler, a person of wide curiosity but the master of no disciplines. Is that a good place to be at the midpoint of my life? What the heck. This isn't the only life I'll ever have on this planet. I may meet up with SHE in a future incarnation, *n'est pas*?

Chapter Eight

October

Up till now I haven't painted myself as a procrastinator. I suppose I was procrastinating about disclosing that essential fact. I'm slow to digest important events and material. A couple of weeks later I felt a need to talk again with Tom Nishinaka. It's as though the thoughts of SHE were communicating with me during my sleep and planting a suspicion that all was not right.

I phoned Susan and she said there had been no word from SHE. She promised to alert me immediately if any clues might arise that could be followed in any direction.

Tom's phone had an answering machine that said no units are available, but if you leave your name and phone number he'll put it on a waiting list or send an application. I would have to drive over and knock on his door. I followed up four times -- driving over and parking in his assigned parking space, which should have told me right there that he was not inside, and he never answered his door bell. Each time added more urgency to that creepy feeling on the hairs on the back of my neck.

The funny thing was, the old Maxima was not there either. Was Susan still driving it? Did she take it to work or has she transferred to another school district this semester? Not really my business, though. Tom was out on some errand, I suppose. I returned to our *pied-a-terre* in Beverly.

MMM: the rest of this chapter was dictated to me by Jay, and I hope that I got it right. Actually for the last part I used a tape recorder when I realized it was going to be lengthy.

In the mid-west we call the October heat wave Indian summer. Frost or cold weather followed by a good warm spell turns the leaves on the trees to gorgeous yellows, browns, reds, and greens. Los Angeles gets the heat treatment also. A furnace type blast comes directly from the desert on strong hot winds called Santa Anas.

I put on the same swim trunks that I purchased in May and went to our apartment swimming pool to cool off. I prefer it when I can swim laps or both lengths underwater without surfacing or worrying about bumping into anyone else swimming or diving. There was one old fellow doing laps so I ducked my head underwater in the shallow end, climbed out, and decided to lie on the chaise until the pool cleared.

In my marine corps training I was instructed in the use of shotguns in addition to the regular assortment of personal war weapons such as the .45 sidearm, the M-1 and the Browning Automatic Rifle (BAR). We used shotguns as guards at the brig while supervising work details.

Once in my life I actually fainted from heat stroke. We were working prisoners chopping weeds along a railroad track outside the base during a blazing hot day in the August sun.

I gave my group of prisoners extra rest breaks when we could find some shade, and of course we carried plenty of water. When a prison bus came to pick us up, the driver was a hard case who did not allow the windows on his pristine-for-inspection bus to be rolled down.

The prisoners were very vocal about this oppressive greenhouse sauna on wheels but the driver was intransigent and he outranked me. We got them back to their brig and into another guard's custody. After they cleared the bus I stepped down and collapsed on the deck from heat stroke.

That was not something I would recall unless it bore some relationship to this story and here's how it fits: On this very hot day in October by the apartment pool I started to feel light headed, much as I felt that day long ago in the prison bus. I had napped briefly on the chaise with a towel over my head and upper body, my legs in the shadow of a chaise nearby. In retrospect maybe there wasn't enough oxygen under the towel. Anyway I stood up kind of groggy, shrugged off the towel and lurched toward the water.

I heard the click of a shotgun from a corner of the pool area. There were no other people around. That sound is an attention focuser. It conveys a picture of large cardboard shells full of pellets going into a chamber ready to explode havoc on the soft flesh of any living thing in its path. Oddly enough, the quieter the sound of a click, the more menacing it seems. It resonates somewhere in the eardrums and auditory nerves speeding to the brain.

The pool was only a few feet away. I wanted to reach that cool water for two reasons. The first reason was to cool down because I was sweating again and suffering from the sun's heat. I headed for the shallow end hoping to coax the water into quickly quenching my light headed feeling. The second reason was, if anyone accidentally or deliberately with malice had me in their sights, I figured instinctively, the water would offer some protection from the blast of shot, slowing it down or stopping it within a few inches under water.

My feet rushed my panicked body forward to the edge of the pool, but at some point before hitting the water my lower back splattered blood and flesh and my next thought was: oh, no, this is going to be a really big mess. They are going to have to drain this pool now. Sorry.

I think the sound of the blast reached my ears less than a second before the pain in my body acknowledged the pellets so they must have came at subsonic speed. Now that I think about it my brain must have been super focused to snapshot the event and recall it for me now.

Just like that time in the guards at the brig I passed out. One giant difference though: The paramedics from the base fire station revived me with oxygen and I was able to walk again. This time I woke up being strapped on a gurney and loaded into an ambulance. They gave me a shot to help me sleep some more and the next time I awoke it was in a hospital bed.

Mitsuko was there beside me. Her face told me the whole story. I didn't need to read the chart at the end of bed. I said, "I've been hoping to finish my Mind Your Business manuscript but the ending hasn't come to me, yet."

Mitsi replied, "You are still waiting for a big finish for your Hugh Hefner biopic script also. Why aren't you suggesting we finish that one, and get it ready to pitch?"

She was referring to my 120 page story boards where my spin is to take a Hef-like character called Harley Hume and put him through a midlife crisis in which he wishes to atone for his shabby treatment of lovely, but intellectually challenged young ladies. It would picture him taking up public service, and meeting a high school sweetheart or his ex-wife in the process that just might develop into a meeting of minds and bodies.

I honestly think Hef would welcome such a project out of Hollywood and would lend all kinds of helpful details if we could only get through his outer office staff. Naturally they have a vested interested in retaining the status quo.

I countered. "This isn't a film script. It's a novel and dependent on real life situations, not Hollywood predictable endings. That script and a few others depended on an unworkable plan. And as ye know, me bonnie lassie, the best laid plans of mice and men *oft gang aglee*. Even faster in the modern world than when Bobby Burns wrote them eons ago."

The first seven and a half chapters of Mind Your Own Business are ready to go. I'm beginning to worry that book stores might put it into the wrong section, though, thinking it is non-fiction advice for shop owners. My outline called for nine chapters, but I guess we won't make it, will we? Finish the novella if you can. Go through my notes in the word processor and choose one of the alternative endings that rings true to you and make it the final chapter.

Maybe the title should be Mind Your Own Garden, eh? If we meet each other on the other side of this one I may still be curious myself about Tom, Susan, SHE, and Nick. So make some mental notes, eh?

> MMM: Jay's notes at the end of his manuscript included trial final chapters depending on where he thought new clues to the missing girl's whereabouts might lead. I chose the following admittedly sketchy chapter to wind up his novel as Chapter Nine. I stashed some of his unused notes in an Appendix.

Chapter Nine

Late October

All things come to he who waits. I waited and the resolution finally came to dissolve my emotional entanglement from the young lady. The resolution was this: SHE had chosen Tom after all and Tom knew it. His heartbreak was an act, a sham which I should have recognized. They both knew she needed to get free from her marriage first. It should have been obvious to me, but I was too close to it to see it.

SHE and Tom perpetrated a hoax by renting a modest apartment over there in Nevada for her to establish residency before filing for divorce. She returned to Santa Monica with Tom and Susan, so that Susan would have plausible deniability of their actions. Of course! It makes sense. If there was any danger at all it must reside strictly with Tom and no innocent parties such as Susan or me.

Then, hoping to keep Susan in the dark, she flew back to Las Vegas, as if leaving Tom and Susan behind, going into some new relationship, taking a taxi to her new digs over there. Yeah, digs with Tom exclusively. That's why Tom has been so hard to catch in person at the apartment or on the phone. He was spending some time out of town, eh? He probably drove their Maxima over there for SHE to use and flew back to Los Angeles, accounting for the missing automobile in his apartment parking lot.

That part I could put together myself and understand, but Tom embellished the scheme a bit more. After establishing the residency, as soon as the divorce papers were filed, SHE was sent up to Washington State to stay at his brother's truck farm up there east of Yakima.

His exact words to me were: "What better place to cool off a heated situation?"

I've always associated Washington State with the Delicious variety of apples. It added beauty to the story, imagining the delicious young lady posing for snapshots among the ripe red apples, posing on a ladder picking a perfect specimen as if it isn't all mechanical these days!

Apples need a cold winter in order to perform their fruit magic. I have tried planting apple trees in the Los Angeles area and they simply cannot endure our heat and/or lack of humidity. We can grow some in the higher elevations out by Yucaipa. Mitsi and I often drive visitors out there to Oak Glen to pick up fresh picked apples or fresh squeezed cider and other goodies.

Yucaipa would have been my choice for a hideout, but then I don't have a brother up near Yakima to serve as a bodyguard. Tom has learned that you can't be too careful in this life. You need to guard what you prize the most.

And because SHE came to America as the husband of that drummer guy she may need to leave the country and re-enter to get square with her visa. She could easily cross into Canada, visit the American consulate in Vancouver, and then re-enter the U.S. via Washington State, whenever it becomes convenient.

As of this writing, though, Tom hasn't indicated if he'll be selling the apartments and moving to Washington State himself, or if he plans to bring his bride back into this area eventually where something accidental might happen.

If I was Nick I would not give up easily. Nick might take the loss gracefully, but in my experience, the rich and powerful are not graceful. And who knows what will happen when her husband receives the legal papers from Nevada? For that matter who knows how many hearts she's broken.

MMM: Per Jay's instructions I've fleshed out his notes thus:

It could even have been her father or brother who came here on visitor's visas who decided to shoot someone on general principles before going home empty handed. We don't even know that there is any connection at all between the shooter and me and/or SHE.

Billy Pilgrim in Vonnegut's Slaughterhouse Five gets shot and killed thirty or forty years later by someone who only imagined he had been slighted by Billy.

The only thing that is clear is that it was a mistake to discharge a weapon around the swimming pool and mistakes don't always have neat motives. Maybe the perpetrator was unfamiliar with the firearm and thought the safety was on. I'll never know.

Although I haven't actually heard the following from the girl's own mouth I'm sure SHE would have said, "Sakura Gardens turned out to be the large house of my dreams. It is elegant, Tom has nice tenants, and it is well located. If it is possible to live there I would love it, but Tom has promised to recreate it elsewhere if I am his wife."

In my view Tom would assume my greatest fantasy life now that he's a reformed gambler, with a perfect wife, perfect garden, *n'est pas*? If they decide to settle in Santa Monica and I am called upon to sing at Tom's next birthday celebration, I will change the fugue words from 'Brother Tom' to 'Lucky Tom.'

We were created in God's image, but not intended to share his omniscience. I cannot say definitively that there is a new couple in this world that adds to its livability but I have that hope. Not knowing the future makes life interesting. When we get there, will Heaven offer our souls only static obeisance and repetitive hymns? Samuel Clemens seemed to think so. Could it be a place of monotonous sameness for eternity? Or did God create man with free will so that there would be some unpredictability in His Mankind/Earth experiment? Sure, that's it! We are God's novel!

The End

Appendix
Posthumous

My husband knew he was dying. The shotgun destroyed both kidneys and damaged enough other adjacent tissues that dialysis machines or transplants would not be able to save him. He said he'd seen the same situation in a film with Richard Todd, Ronald Reagan and Patricia Neal called The Hasty Heart. You know your body is filling up with toxins and it's only a matter of time until you faint and don't wake up.

I assisted him with Chapter Eight at the hospital. It seemed important it him. He told me how to find, cut and paste Chapter Nine (he didn't call it that by number) in his notes on the word processor. He had enough of an idea there to tie up the loose ends and finish the story.

Jay wavered over the use of Cufflett's name in his novel. It was already a disguised name for the man he dined with at Benihana's among other places, and he was leaning toward a better cover name, perhaps using 'Jacques Fromagier,' who might be a Canadian citizen, lending some distance to the actual person. He told me the real name of the Cufflett character and I found his card with the post office address to give to the police.

I showed this manuscript to a police detective who investigated the shooting of my husband. He said it cannot admissible as a clue to the crime since it is self labeled a novel. He said Nicholas Cufflett could be a composite of several men Jay knew and the manuscript doesn't name Cufflett as the assailant in any case.

The detective contacted Cufflett, however, to see if the drummer at that Malibu party had an alibi for the time of the shooting. Cufflett denied arranging for the music at the Malibu party and said he did not know any drummers who played such gigs. It was a dead end. You might think it would have been easy for the police to track and query the drummer/husband of SHE from news reports of that garden party but if so, they never advised me one way or the other.

I wondered about SHE myself but Jay left no clues as to her verifiable identity. A good detective might deduce what day she applied for a driver's license and then scan all the Asian names in the Santa Monica DMV office on that date, and check them out, but this case was not a priority. Even if they found her and her husband, there would be no connection to the shooter unless it was him and he had a shotgun in his closet that showed it had been fired recently. Even that would not be good evidence because shotguns scatter little pellets--- no rifling marks to identify it with those in Jay's kidneys.

Susan and Tom have been clueless as well. It seems likely that SHE has moved away from this area, perhaps with her husband or someone else. Probably doesn't even know of Jay's demise.

AFFIDAVIT

City of XXXXX XXXXXX
County of XXX XXXXXXX
State of California

XXXX XXXXXXXX, first being duly sworn, deposes and says:

1. That his name is XXXX XXXXXXXX.

2. That he has met Jay G. Miller at social gatherings on the West Side.

3. That the Beverly Hills Police Department questioned him about a relationship with a recent young woman immigrant. He strongly denies having any such relationship.

4. As a personal favor to Professor Moriyama, he has read the novel titled, Mind Your Own Business, by Jay G. Miller. That he did not recognize himself in the Nick Cufflett character in any way.

5. That he had dined with Miller at Benihana's but they had not gone fishing together or socialized accompanied by any females at any time.

6. That he has no formal or informal connections with any musical groups nor provided them for private events

7. That he does not know any musicians or drummers personally with their addresses, or phone numbers.

8. That further, affiant sayeth naught.

Sworn this day, December 21, 1979

Xxxx Xxxxxxxx
_____

MMM: I edited out the following on the topic of male self destructive lust because it didn't seem to fit.

Chapter One. One of the impressionable MGM films I saw as a callow youth was The Egyptian. Edmund Purdom was a physician named Sinuhe in a poor neighborhood of Cairo in Old Testament days. His retired father was also a doctor but idealistically lived and practiced in their impoverished neighborhood. The young doctor meets and becomes infatuated with a courtesan played by an exotic actress named Bella Darvi. She tells him honestly that she is too expensive for him, that he has no chance of receiving her favors. Still, she promises to give him her treasures if he will first bring her all of his treasures.

Sinuhe has very few earthly goods but he sells all that he has, including his medical instruments, and brings it to the courtesan. She throws the coins into her hope chest but tells him he is holding out treasures from her. He says 'no, I've given you everything I own!' She says, 'I know you possess your parents immortality graves when they die. If you bring me those deeds (negotiable instruments?), I will show you the perfection of love!'

Without that legal burial papyrus his parents lose their gateway to everlasting life! So, this young doctor, hopelessly obsessed with beauty fit for a Pharoah, is willing to sacrifice his own soul and the souls of his parents for one taste of exquisite pleasure. He fetches the deeds and brings them to her. She takes them and puts them into her hope chest and says, 'Goodbye Sinuhe.' He protests, 'But wait, wait! You promised if I did this, you would show me the perfection of love!' She smiles and says, 'Perfection is when it is over. I don't want to play with you anymore.' Sinuhe does not appreciate the sophistry of that explanation and its denouement. He flies into a rage and dispatches her to a place where those burial documents might be useful to the executor of her estate.

Then he purchases new burial insurance for his parents in exchange for years of indentured labor in the City of the Dead, preparing bodies for mummification and incidentally learning more about human anatomy. After paying that debt he goes into exile and travels the world learning medicinal arts and returns from exile under the protection of a boyhood friend, General Victor Mature, son of a cheesemaker, after a military coup. Jean Simmons is still waiting for him.

Purdom also played The Prodigal Son in another movie. He played The Student Prince using Mario Lanza's voice in a third MGM film. He must have had an aura of prodigal playboys to have won three similar roles.

> MMM: There was more of the Egyptian story and although we haven't seen it advertised on cable television, you might seek it out and enjoy the performances of Peter Ustinov, Jean Simmons, Michael Wilding. Gene Tierney and Tommy Rettig (from Lassie). Another long paragraph that I edited out quotes Michael Wilding, as the poisoned dying pharaoh who tried to begin a religion based on One God, with an eloquent appeal to humanity to share the earth equally with love for one another, the One True God, etc. As he expires Victor Mature, the new Pharoah mourns, 'Poor soul. He was mad to the end!'

Notes for the novel

Possible endings – final chapter:

1. SHE realizes that leaving her husband after arrival here within the same year will cause problems with her visa. She could get deported. She phones her parents and they beg her to come home and start over. They never liked her husband either. They contact a family friend to pick her up and buy the air ticket.

2. SHE is finally located by Nick after discovering she left her husband. He goes to her apartment and tells her that her husband if looking for her and threatened to use a gun to use on anyone who has played a part in estranging her from him. She thinks, 'that could be Jay, Tom, or Susan -- I better protect my friends and go with Nick who has the resources to hide me, relocate me, until things cool off.' What other choice is there?

3. SHE gets tracked down by her husband to Sakura Gardens. He knocks on her door and tells her he'll report her to Immigration if she doesn't come home. He demands that she accompany him to San Francisco to stay with his brother while he looks for permanent work in that area. He demands that she never see or contact any of those people who kidnapped her from him.

4. SHE and Susan perpetrated a hoax by ---

5. SHE and Tom perpetrated a hoax by renting a modest ---

****

Acknowledgment of cover art:
BigStockPhoto.com #2838299 Zen Studio

Acknowledgment of two pages recycled from:
Alternative Birthday Serenades and Anthems, paperback $6
A Grist of Millers Short Stories and Tall Tales, paperback $9
Akapella Akademy 8132 Firestone Blvd. #932, Downey CA 90241

****

Classic anecdote re: human powers of perception:
An elephant is slender and sharp like a spear said the sage who touched the tusk.

An elephant is long, round, and flexible like a snake said the sage who touched the trunk.

An elephant is like a leather screen said the sage who touched the ear.

An elephant is round and solid like tree trunk said the sage who touched a leg.

An elephant is wide and flat like a wall said the sage who touched its side.

****

Epitaph:

Re: Charles Foster Kane's 'Rosebud -- Rosebud.'   On his tombstone Jay wants his epitaph to read 'the honeys --- the honeys ---' It's his homage to Orson Welles, Joseph Conrad, Marlon Brando, and Jude Narita.

****

Gandhi's (the Mahatma) Seven Deadly Sins:

- Wealth without Work

- Pleasure without Conscience

- Science without Humanity

- Knowledge without Character

- Politics without Principle

- Commerce without Morality

- Worship without Sacrifice

****

Gravitas:

MMM: There were too many anecdotes so I abbreviated to 'who & where'; deleted 'when, what, why, and how':

Anecdotes about personal encounters with VIPs for possible use in a story to highlight a point. Here is one sample:

"I stood side by side with five-star General of the Army Omar Bradley in the urinals at the Hollywood Bowl. He had some attendants with a wheel chair taking care of him but some things a man has to do for himself."

Steve Allen: at his theater next to the Farmers Market
James Baldwin: speaking at a church in Watts in the 70s
Mayor Tom Bradley: guests at ACLU garden party West Covina
Governor Edmund (Jerry) Brown: garden party Azusa
Marlon Brando: fair housing demonstration at Dominguez Hills
Carol Burnett: at the taping in Television City
Attorney General Tom Clark: book signing and Cal State L.A.
Van Cliburn: at Pasadena Civic Auditorium
His Holiness the Dalai Lama XIV: at Claremont Colleges
Cecil B. DeMille: at Paramount Studio - The Ten Commandments
Jane Fonda: garden party in San Dimas
Charlton Heston: at Paramount Studios sponsored by USO
Bob Hope: curbside at the Music Center
Eric Idle: with his daughter in Dr. Bloore's waiting room
State Senator Sheila Kuehl: playing "Ma" in stage play prison
Dr. Armand Hammer: my employer at Oxy Petroleum
S. I. Hayakawa: answered my question at Beverly Hills High
Col. Anthony Herbert: book signing, most decorated SOLDIER!
Rafer Johnson: Mt. San Antonio College track meet, decathlon
Martin Luther King Jr.:   speaking at Presbyterian Church in Pasadena
Burt Lancaster: when he appeared at Steve Allen's show
Norman Lear, warming up the audience at Maude
Liberace: L.A. Home Show and Las Vegas show room
Bob Mathias: Camp Pendleton USMC base
Jayne Meadows: when I was employed at So. Cal S & L
Gary Merrill: chat about Jonathan Livingston Seagull
Prime Minister Kiichi Miyazawa: his house guest in Shibuya
Lord Louis Mountbatten: speaking at Cal State L.A.
David & Igor Oistrakh, in concert at Shrine Auditoreum
Tony Randall: during taping of the Odd Couple
Nelson Rockefeller: luncheon in Rock Island, the Rock Club

Roy Rogers: Rock Island train depot
Mickey Rooney: used Jay as foil, Sugar Babies at the Pantages
Rod Serling: guest at his Pacific Palisades home
Upton Sinclair: speaking at meeting hall, L.A. Exposition Park
Tom Smothers: garden party at Pacific Palisades
Dr. Benjamin Spock: house party in Pasadena
Isaac Stern: back stage, Bridges Auditorium, Claremont Colleges
Adlai Stevenson: in his Springfield Ill. office with other cub scouts
Barbra Streisand: in concert The Forum, Inglewood
Danny Thomas, curbside in Beverly Hills
President Harry Truman, back of a train at Moline depot
John Wayne: Rock Island train depot

Jay had personal notes from: Isaac Asimov, Norman Lloyd, James Michener, Pierre Salinger, Yma Sumac, Marty Ingels & Shirley Jones. He wrote an anecdote about a phone call from Alana Ladd Jackson

****

Great Retort:

Jude Narita in her one woman play has a retort to some bozo who insulted her as yellow skinned. She replied, 'No, I don't think so! I've studied it and it's not yellow; it's the color of honey -- sweet, tasty, honey.' And she was right!

****

Idioms in the text with Jay's interpretation for readers:

alfresco	Italian	fresh air, outside dining
ars gratia artis	Latin	art for the sake of art

au contraire	French	contrary, the opposite
b.s.	Euphemism	bla-bla stuff
bonjour tristesse	French	Hello sadness
crème de la crème	French	best, cream of the cream
daimyo	Japanese	lord, boss
dojo	Japanese	martial arts building
et les autres	French	and others
faux	French	false, phony
faux pas	French	social mistake
forte	French	best feature
gaijin	Japanese	foreign born
haku-jin	Japanese	caucasian born
hors d'oeurves	French	finger food
iyashi	Japanese	lowest class
judenfrei	German	jew-free
judoka	Japanese	judo person
mon frere	French	my brother
n'est pas?	French	isn't it so?
numero uno	Italian	number one
pied-a-terre	French	dwelling, apartment
raison d'etre	French	reason for being
sakura	Japanese	cherries
sotto voce	Italian	softly, not to be overheard
touché	French	ouch, you got me

****

Notes for Screenplays

<u>The Return of the Dragon Lady</u>: like the Phantom she inherits the position from her mother. All her followers revere her as if she is the original and perpetually ageless phenomenon. Her mission is to relocate

most of Hong Kong to Catalina Island when it reverts to Communist China.

The Admiral, a retired Navy Admiral paints scenes from memory of World War II Pacific ports where he served on supply ships. One painting of island harbors includes a hillside cemetery where the body of a Japanese admiral is buried in full samurai armor. This painting interests a Japanese student at U of Wash who contacts the Black Ocean Society to offer a possible clue to the island where looted diamonds were stashed en route to their conquered homeland.

The Falls, a remake of 1953 Marilyn Monroe film *Niagara* by a Japanese film company with an Asian femme fatale. There are dual roles for the main characters as the producer/director and his staff put spins on the roles of the Charles Brackett production. For example, the Japanese production team also acts as prepilgrim natives in the Maid of the Mist foreshadowing prologue.

> MMM: The Falls was Jay's portrayal of a nagging shrewish Japanese wife as a private joke with me in my very humble opinion.

****

Red Ingle and the Natural Seven:

A preachment, dear friends, you're about to receive,
on John Barleycorn, nicotine, and the temptations of Eve.......
(singing) Oh once I was happy and had a good life
I had enough money to last me for life
I met with a gal and we went on a spree
She taught me to smoke and drink whiskey
Cigarettes and whiskey and wild wild women
They'll drive you crazy they'll drive you insane

Cigarettes and whiskey and wild wild women
They'll drive you crazy they'll drive you insane
Cigareets is a blot on the whole human race
A man is a monkey with one in his face
That's my definition, believe me dear brother
A fire on one end, a fool on the t'other

****

Words in the novel that may have been coined by Jay:

forefounders   The colonists who broke with the mother country and established the United States.

prepilgrim natives – indigenous people of Canada and USA before Plymouth Rock.

pescatory - I couldn't find it in the dictionary but it's obviously derived from Italian *pescatore* regarding fishing.

Zen conundrum

Man can easily explain what he has not experienced. It is what he experiences that he cannot explain.   Sharol Watson, NYU Student

****

Haiku epitaph
Snow now covers Jay
The honey --- the honeys --- Oh
God, just out of reach

Printed in the United States
by Baker & Taylor Publisher Services